Books by TLW Savage

Heroes come in all sizes

Tuffy

Pooh and P'Nut

First Test Hexology (Six books)

Alex Twice Abducted

Alex Terrified Hero

Alex Inner Voice

Alex String Sword

Alex & Hheilea Challenge the Darkness

Alex & the Crystal of Jedh...coming soon

Pronunciations
And Definitions

- **Annie** –

  Annie is a very loving and friendly dog. Her breed is newfie. She is very big.

- **Artificial Intelligence** –

  Artificial Intelligence (AI) is a set of technologies allowing computers to perform a number of things. In some ways, it makes the computers seem intelligent, but they are still just programs doing what they've been designed to do. As artificial intelligence gets better, it is harder to tell the difference between the artificial intelligence and real intelligence.

- **Boots** –

  He is a black house cat and the friend of Sally.

- **Dark Matter** –

  Dark matter is a purely theoretical substance. In this book world, it is real and has the unusual effect of making some living organisms able to play with the laws of physics.

- **Frise** – Fer ēz

  She is a cute and very friendly little white dog. She is a bichon frise.

- **Fuego** – Fuā gō

  He is a very temperamental hummingbird and only 3 inches long. He is a Calliope hummingbird.

- **Incessantly** –

    Without stopping.

- **Izzy or Isabella** – Iz ē

    She is a human eighteen-year-old, and she is an old classmate of Noah's.

- **Laws of Physics** –
    Physics is full of laws describing all kinds of fun, amazing, and sometimes dangerous things. Newton's Law of Motion is one example describing how objects move, but it doesn't cover how things move in quantum physics.

- **Noah** – No-uh

    He is a nerd. He is more at ease with animals than with humans.

- **NGOs** –

    Non-governmental organizations have no fixed or formal definition. They are generally defined as nonprofit entities independent of governmental influence or control, but they may receive government funding.

- **Pooh** –

    Pooh is a black bear. He is only about nine months old. He is light brown and likes wearing a ragged red shirt just like the fictional bear, Winnie the Pooh.

- **P'Nut** –

    P'Nut is an Eastern Gray Squirrel. He loves watching movies with his friends and has dreams of being a superhero.

- **Raptor** –

    The raptors of this book are not the extinct raptors. These raptors are birds of prey like an eagle, a hawk, a falcon, or an owl.

- **Rattled or Rattling** –

    Rattling is the act of pouring out an excess of words. It commonly happens when one does not know what to say but feels the need to say something. Someone has rattled if they have done this. It is talking, but just making words without trying to communicate anything.

- **Quantum** –

    A simple definition of quantum used in this book is that quantum is referring to both the study of how matter and energy function at the atomic and subatomic levels and quantum is referring to those very strange ways matter and energy function at the atomic and subatomic levels. How things act at the quantum level both determine our reality and are responsible for some very strange things that hardly seem real. It is really mind-bending stuff and has done amazing things for us with new technology.

- **Sally** –

    He's a raven, but he was imprinted by a young human girl and was raised with a cat. Sally fortunately was partially imprinted by his original raven parents, but he's mixed up. He thinks he's a human and likes cats, but at another level knows he's a raven.

- **Self-deprecation** –

    Being modest about yourself or criticizing yourself. In this usage, it was making modest statements about themselves.

- **Siberian Tiger** –

    They are the largest living tigers, but because of illegal hunting and lack of prey, adults are smaller than they used to be. When considering the three-foot long tails, males can get almost ten feet long.

- **Strong Force** –

     Tigger plays with this fundamental force to be able to disintegrate non-living substances. In physics, the STRONG FORCE refers to a fundamental interaction that binds quarks together to form protons and neutrons, essentially holding the atomic nucleus together. That's how he makes holes in things.

- **Tuffy** –

     He is a male, red-tailed hawk, but he was imprinted by bald eagles that accidently adopted him. He thinks he's an eagle.

- **Tigger** – tig r; pronounced like tear plus a c sound like in pierce

     He is an almost seven-foot long tiger. He is named after Tigger of Pooh fame by the little dog Frise.

Pooh and P'Nut

TLW Savage

ISBN-13: 9781947133099

ISBN-10: 1947133099

DEDICATION

This book is dedicated to my fans and animal lovers everywhere. My fans enjoyment of my previous animal book Pooh and all of his friends have been a great source of entertainment for many. Hopefully, this additional tale about a bear named Pooh and his friends will be that and more for you. Thank you.

I also dedicate this book to my wonderful wife, Debbie, whose forbearance for years with my writing struggles allowed for the opportunity to continue to fruition. All of your support and belief in me and in this project has been instrumental in its success.

One fan Abraham suggested I include a goat. There was an opportunity to do so in this book. Thank you for the suggestion.

What follows is the best thanks I can give. Please read on. Laugh, cry, and think. Be amazed and fascinated. Enjoy and at the end of the book have a good life. I love you.

CONTENTS CHAPTER

Prelude
Pooh, P'Nut, and Annie

Pooh

In 1925, A. A. Milne and E. H. Shepard created the wonderful "Winnie the Pooh." In years gone by, I and others have enjoyed their creation. Also, I have been inspired by their characterization of Pooh. In my own story, I refer to another fictional bear as Pooh. This bear has some resemblance to the original bear, but only some. I hope this bear, my Pooh, also connects to you, and you enjoy him and his story as much as I did in creating it for you.

P'Nut

In 2017, a baby, male Eastern Gray Squirrel lost its mother to a car. A man found and rescued the baby. Many other baby squirrels have been rescued and released back to the wild, but this squirrel ended up living a domesticated life. Unfortunately, in 2024, in the state they lived in, that was not legal. The law is to protect the animals and the people. In this case, the government took P'Nut and killed him. The people caring for P'Nut were, of course, devastated.

I love animals, and this story about a squirrel killed by a government bureaucracy assigned the task of protecting animals spoke to me. I have also wanted to use a squirrel as a character. I hope you enjoy my P'Nut as much as I do in this story.

Annie

This is also a story about a dog Annie. Annie was a dog I cared for. Technically, we owned her, but I didn't consider her a thing I owned. Unfortunately, dogs live for just a short time. I still miss my friend, Annie. It has been enjoyable for me to bring her back to life if only in print and to share her with you.

This story also has the original characters from the previous book, Tuffy, and in particular, a pyro hummingbird and a teenage girl are in this story from the previous one.

This is about their journeys and a goal. Now, let's enjoy their story.

Chapter One

P-Nut

Eastern Gray Squirrels have a hearing range two-and-a-half times that of humans. They hear higher frequencies similar to dogs, and they have an incredibly good sense of smell and a very good sense of touch. They can tell good and bad acorns apart by their sense of touch. Apparently, according to the fictional story of Willy Wonka, they can also tell a bad kid from a good kid by touch.

Squirrels are hyper. They respond much faster than humans can. To a squirrel, humans move almost as slow as a sloth.

P'Nut, an Eastern Gray Squirrel, incessantly flicked his shorter than normal tail and stomped his feet at the intruders. The little squirrel wore the suit jacket he loved to wear one day a week, and usually, he only got to wear it for a short part of the day. The jacket had a fake white shirt. The shirt only consisted of the ends of the sleeves, white collar and a bit more, and the entire fake shirt was sewn to the jacket. P'Nut'd been warning the intruders to leave the house and free his friend. P'Nut was perched on a high-shelf next to some pictures. There was a picture of him in his *James Blonde* pose, and another of him wearing a cross. P'Nut loved watching James Blonde defeat evil in the movies.

James Blonde always succeeded in his missions. *My mission is to get these bad people to leave.*

These men were evil, P'Nut was sure of that. He looked down at the five strangers in his home. Each of them held a pole with a net on the other end. The strangers had barged into the house. They hadn't spoken nice. P'Nut bit people who were not nice. *What would James Blonde do?* P'Nut had dreamed of fighting evil, but now that he had evil to deal with, he wasn't so sure.

After a long half-a-second of waiting, the little gray squirrel scolded them again. "I don't want to go with you. You're evil. You're very bad." The men were bad, but a horrible smell really frightened P'Nut. He didn't know what the smell was, but it frightened him. *It must be something very, very evil.* His friend, his human-food-slave, had told P'Nut to get away, to escape, but that meant going outside. He heard the dog barking outside.

Why can't these people just let me live with my friends? What's wrong with that? I don't want to leave.

P'Nut shuddered at the thought of going outside. Outside frightened him more than the evil smell. That dog, Fido, was the cause of his tail being shorter than normal. P'Nut studied the pattern the men made in the room, the length of their poles, the chandelier, the furniture, the three video cameras, and the marbles he'd already knocked onto the floor. P'Nut also enjoyed watching *Jackie Chan* movies. That man used everything around him in his battles against evil. P'Nut's large eyes gleamed at the thought of how the marbles fit into his plan. If the men moved to just the right positions, he should be able to... P'Nut had already noticed the big bowl with flour, but he checked its location again. The woman friend had started to make cookies just before the bad people arrived. P'Nut remembered again the mess flour could make. *Where did flour come from? I've tipped over a bowl before. For best effect, I'll need the men piled up right—*

As P'Nut thought, he kept scolding them. "You're bad. Leave me alone. I'm warning you for the last time. Leave. Leave me—"

A man with a grizzled beard interrupted his scolding. "Yes, I am a big, bad man. Look, little rat, you have a choice. Either you come with us or—" The man sliced a finger across his throat.

Another, smaller, younger man, interrupted. "We aren't supposed to kill the squirrel. With this new thing living behind everyone's ears, we understand animals, and they understand our commands. It's easier than before. We're supposed to rescue it." He spoke slower. "Little squirrel, we're here to give you your freedom and help you live outside."

A shudder ran down P'Nut's spine at the idea of living outside. *This guy's crazy. Is that worse than evil?*

The bearded man also had a loose, untucked shirt. He poked the small man. "You're a naïve fool. What do you think we're going to do with the rat after we get it?"

P'Nut scolded them. "Evil people, bad people, crazy people go away. I'm warning you. I'm warning you." This plan needed to work. Already, the chasing and setting up his plan had worn him out. *They need to leave. I need to eat, drink, and rest.*

Another man said, "Come on, this isn't rocket science. All we have to do is net it, and put it into the cage." He waved his net at P'Nut.

In response, P'Nut leaped to the chandelier. It swung crazily. He heard a noise from the ceiling. The men yelled. All the while, the little squirrel chattered at them. "You can't catch me. You can't catch me. You're too slow. You're stupid and slow." The insults worked as he'd expected.

All of the men jumped into action. They waved their nets at him. The poles clanged into each other and hit the chandelier. More noises came from the ceiling. In a frenzy of movement, P'Nut jumped from the chandelier. *There are five heads and five nets, one for each.*

P'Nut dove into the shirt of the bearded man. "I warned you."

He ran laps inside the shirt not worried at all about how sharp his claws were. *He wants to kill me. I can do this. I am a little James Blonde.*

The man yelled, "He's got a hold on me."

"Grab him."

With a surprisingly high-pitched voice the bearded man pleaded. "Help me. Oh, help me. I'm sorry I threatened you. Please stop."

P'Nut felt the man fall to his knees. Quick as a flash, the little squirrel darted out the bottom of his untucked shirt.

The poles clanged into each other above him. P'Nut heard the solid clunk of heads hitting heads. Leaping and darting, the little squirrel avoided the staggering feet.

"He's on the floor."

"Now, we've got him."

Poles and waving arms filled the air above P'Nut. "No, you don't. Leave me alone. Leave me alone."

P'Nut was tempted to run up inside a baggy pant leg, but he had to stick to his plan. The temptation was too great. Quick as a flash, P'Nut zipped up inside the pant leg. The crotch stank and was tighter than he'd expected. *This would be easier without my jacket.* P'Nut scratched his way past. The man yelled and tugged at his pants.

The man screamed, "I've got a weed eater in my Fruit-of-the-Looms. Mercy, somebody help me."

By the time the man had finished screaming for help, P'Nut had already zipped down and out the other pant leg. He was just in time to see another of the men facing the man he'd just terrorized. The man had a leg drawn back and he said, "Hold still, I'll get him."

That man kicked and the other screamed even louder. P'Nut had never heard someone scream so loud. P'Nut ran around on the floor threatening them. "I'm going to get you. I'm going to get you."

The bearded one cried, "Don't let him get into your pants. Step on him. Please, don't let him get me again."

The men started dancing a jig. The room shook from the five men stamping, hopping, and screaming. The floor creaked and groaned. For a moment, P'Nut thought one of them was praying, but he wasn't sure. He didn't understand much about praying. Maybe, he was just pleading for help. P'Nut's movements were getting slower. Each moment brought him closer to getting stomped on by a boot. *I don't like the idea of getting stomped on.* It was time to get the plan back on track.

The men were almost at the marbles. To get them out of the house, P'Nut needed to completely demoralize them.

"You're bad men. I warned you." P'Nut gathered his fading energy. *I can do this. I have to.*

In a flash, P'Nut jumped from the floor, and in quick succession he landed on each man's chest. He said, "You can't catch me. You can't catch me."

The men yelled, "Catch him."

P'Nut went totally berserk. He leapt on a head. He had to wait longer than he wanted. *Boy, these guys are slow.*

P'Nut jumped just before a net descended. He almost missed the next head. That man had netted the first man's head, and at the same time, the man must've stepped onto a marble with a resultant yell and waving of his arms, the man started to fall.

In slow motion, P'Nut jumped from head to head. Each time, he waited and just avoided the net. *I'm slowing. They're getting closer to catching me.* Behind him, the men tugged at their poles, swore, and started falling.

As the last man fell into the pile, the little squirrel leaped. P'Nut remembered about the power of suggestion. "Now, you will pay for bothering us. This is either itching powder or poison. I don't care which it is. You will pay."

His latest threat finished, P'Nut landed on the edge of the bowl. He pulled, throwing his weight into the effort and using his momentum. The bowl flipped into the air. P'Nut scurried along the counter that separated the living room from the kitchen. With another leap, he reached the high shelf and turned. In satisfaction, P'Nut looked back at the result. *Now, I can rest.* The men, covered in a film of white flour, moaned in a pile on the floor. The bowl rolled to a stop and the last of the flour gently fell. *Good, maybe now they'll give up.*

One of the men said, "Don't breathe it in."

P'Nut had an idea. He knew it was a bad idea. Humans didn't like it. *They wanted to kill me. Briefly, he argued with himself.* He heard a slapping sound. *What was that noise?*

The bearded man lay with his head turned so one ear was on top. P'Nut leapt, landed, and bit. He really didn't bite hard. Human skin was so tender. Still, he didn't even draw blood.

Shocked out of his daze, the human screamed, "He bit me."

With a couple of bounds, P'Nut perched back on the highest shelf and watched. His ears twitched and his tail flicked. He shifted back and forth on his feet. *How long before they do something? I can't stand this waiting.* Again, he heard a slapping sound. The need for rest kicked back in, and P'Nut actually stopped moving and just watched. He felt his heart slowing.

The third time he heard the slapping noise, P'Nut looked toward the entry. At first, he couldn't see into the small alcove. It was dark in there. As he looked, he heard a softer, feminine voice speak. "Don't be wimps. Now that he's bitten one of you, we don't need to be as

9

careful about killing him. It's time for my plan."

Something about her voice made his fur crawl.

A short, slender woman stepped into the room from the entry. She stood slowly slapping the side of her thigh-high leather boot with a stick of some sort. For some reason, this person and her soft voice made his heart race in new fear. *This must be their evil boss. The Blonde movies and Jackie Chan movies always had an evil boss, but she doesn't look evil. What can I do? My human friend wanted me to escape, to use my strange vibrating way of moving through things, but that would mean I failed in my mission.*

The squirrel remembered the cat chasing him. P'Nut still didn't know how he'd done what he'd done. *Why did someone let the cat in?* P'Nut had been terrified. When he'd jumped at the window, he hadn't realized until too late that the window wasn't open.

What had happened next had surprised him. He still didn't know how he did it. P'Nut had vibrated so fast he'd been able to pass through the window. He hadn't felt the window at all. P'Nut enjoyed the memory of seeing the cat slam against the window. What had happened outside with the dog had terrified P'Nut. It still terrified him. *Outside is terrible, terrible. I can't go outside.*

The thought of going outside made him start a new plan for dealing with the evil boss. She was just another slow human. At the same time, P'Nut remembered what he'd learned so far about vibrating and what he could do.

The woman stood still except for slowly slapping her boot with the stick. In the same deceptively soft voice, she said, "Let the weasels go."

P'Nut tried to ignore the fear her voice made him feel. *Weasels? Or did she say woozles? What was a woozle or a weasel?* P'Nut debated what a woozle would be. Would it have a trunk or a long tail? What colors would it be? Would they have stripes or polka-dots? His mind raced trying to figure out this new threat.

The men on the floor groaned.

Where have I heard of woozles before? Was it a movie? Vaguely, P'Nut remembered a movie about a little bear. *What was the bear's name? Pooh?* Then, he remembered. *Winnie the Pooh, but what does a bear have to do with woozles?* He remembered the silly bear. *That silly thing wouldn't be any help. No use trying to remember more about that movie.*

Over the moans, P'Nut heard another noise, another quieter and nastier voice. A shudder ran down the little squirrel's back.

"Mine. The prey is mine."

Another, equally blood-curdling voice said, "You can have a leg after I kill it."

From behind the small, delicate woman, three long small creatures flowed like shadows or oil on water. With their short tails, they were as long or longer than P'Nut's body, but smaller.

The size of the creatures didn't fit with their voices. P'Nut didn't recognize what they were, but, by instinct, he knew the little creatures were deadly predators. They each had chestnut brown fur on the top half of their bodies and a lighter cream colored brown on the lower half. *They aren't polka-dotted.*

The tired little squirrel yelled, "Stay away. Stay away."

The little creatures didn't answer. They just kept on coming.

In a voice that wasn't just soft and feminine, the woman said, "Animals are vermin. Kill it."

A shudder ran down P'Nut's back. He recognized the other quality of her voice. It was evil.

The one who hadn't said anything answered, "Thanks for the

11

compliment. It will die."

Chapter Two

Pooh and Honey

Black bears love honey. They also need to eat large amounts of food to grow big and to prepare for hibernation. Bears, like Pooh in this story, can get injured in one or both front paws and, as a result, walk upright most of the time just like a human. That is real, and it looks funny.

Those bears have acute close-up vision, but not good distance vision. Their hearing is twice as good as a human's. Their sense of smell is extremely good and about seven times better than dogs. Also, they are one of the more intelligent mammals. All of that is amazing. Black bears come in colors other than just black, including the light brown of Pooh.

The trouble all began one fine warm summer day. Trouble stalked other people on that day, but in the morning of the day, Pooh knew nothing of the danger or of being a hero.

Pooh watched a butterfly dance in the gentle breeze. He liked watching butterflies. They made him feel peaceful. When he was peaceful, his thoughts wandered.

Pooh thought of himself as a little bear. When the humans who cared for him sat in a chair, Pooh wanted to climb into their laps. *I don't know why they think I'm too big. They say I'm still not quite over one hundred pounds. I wonder what pounds and hundred means, but one anything can't be very big. One has to mean small. One must mean I'm still small, but just a little too big for climbing*

13

into laps, but not too big for making them laugh. They do laugh when I want to climb into their laps, and they say I'm not a big black bear yet.

Pooh wondered why they called him a black bear. He wasn't black. Instead, he was a light brown color which went quite well with his ragged red shirt.

Pooh also remembered how his right front paw hurt if he walked on it. He looked at his paw. *It still hurts to walk on it. Oh well, I can walk on two feet just like humans, and more importantly, both of my front paws work absolutely fine for eating honey.*

Thinking of honey made Pooh hungry. Well, he was always hungry. It just made him notice the hunger. *I love honey. If there's a heaven, it had to have honey.* The slightly under one hundred pound bear smacked his lips and patted his tummy just like he'd been taught. Pooh looked around, but no one brought him any food. He looked at his snack bowl. Pooh couldn't see any food. Just in case his eyes had missed anything, the little bear carefully sniffed around the bowl. His nose could always find what his eyes couldn't see. Pooh didn't find any food.

Where did my family go? A man and his wife had cared for Pooh ever since his mother had died. Pooh thought of them as his mother and father. The thoughts of honey made Pooh think of the neighbor. The little bear looked toward the neighbor's farm. He always had honey.

Pooh liked the farmer. The farmer's name was Peter. Peter was the name of a rabbit in a story his family had read to him. Pooh knew the farmer wasn't a rabbit. So, for the little bear, it seemed strange to call the farmer Peter. Instead, Pooh always called him Farmer.

Listening to stories was a puzzling thing, but Pooh liked thinking about them. They were good to remember. This made Pooh remember more about those stories. *In another book, the Pooh book, the rabbit always has honey. Farmer has the rabbit name. He always has honey. Just like Rabbit in the Pooh book, Farmer always shares honey.*

Winnie the Pooh lived in a hundred acre woods. At least, that's what the book said they'd read to me, but that isn't the truth for me. That Pooh had adventures with his friends. This little bear only had a human dad and mom and one friend, Farmer.

The little bear didn't remember where his family had gone. He did know his family had left him in his pen, so he wouldn't get into trouble while they were gone. Pooh looked at his snack bowl. It was still empty. He thought again of Farmer. Pooh plopped down on his rear. He cried out, "Mom, Dad, where are you? I'm hungry. Can I have a snack, please?"

Pooh tried to listen patiently for a reply. His parents had explained to him how some strange new creature living behind everyone's ears could translate everyone's words. Otherwise, they wouldn't have understood him. They had also taught Pooh to be polite.

The little bear's stomach was not patient. It also did not like being polite. His stomach forced him to smell around his pen. He'd been taught that fences meant he shouldn't go. At one spot, Pooh stopped. The fence didn't go to the ground in that spot. The little bear thought about that spot. *Any fence means stop, but no fence means I can go. Down there is no fence, so I can go. I could put my nose under there.*

Pooh put his nose under the fence. Something about this bothered the little bear, but his stomach said to follow his nose. The little bear pushed and wriggled. In no time at all, Pooh crawled out from under the fence. He looked back at his pen. The fence looked all twisted. Pooh knew fences were not supposed to get twisted. *It must be a bad fence.*

Pooh's nose turned him around and pointed him at Farmer's. Another fence stood in the way. The little bear knew a way in. He walked out to the road. Happily, the Pooh hurried down the road. He thought of honey.

The little bear stopped at the gate to the farmer's home. Pooh'd been taught good bears always stop at gates. His nose told him to keep going. Pooh remembered his pen.

He leaned over and looked down at the bottom of the fence. Unfortunately, it went all the way to the ground. Pooh poked at one spot with a paw. The dirt moved a little. Was there a gap? "Oh bother, I just want a little honey."

At that moment, he heard the farmer. "Pooh? Honey? Oh, no, oh, my, oh no. Oh, my goodness gracious."

Happily, Pooh looked over the gate. He couldn't see the farmer, but he'd heard him or somebody. Pooh liked the farmer. He always treated Pooh nice and gave him a bit of honey. Again, Pooh was tempted to push through the gate, but he remembered how he was supposed to behave. Behaving was hard, but when he did, the treats were good.

In as friendly of a voice as he could muster, Pooh asked, "Is anyone at home?"

There was no answer.

Pooh tried again. "What I said was is 'Is there anyone at home?'"

This time he heard an answer. It sounded like the farmer. "No."

Pooh sat down at the answer. He tried to think. Talking with humans could be hard. They confused Pooh, but the harder he thought the easier it had gotten. This time, the thinking didn't help. Pooh still didn't understand. He tried again. "Isn't there anyone home at all?"

Again, Pooh heard the voice that sounded like the farmer. "Nobody."

Listening hard and trying to understand, he heard more. "Pooh is out of his pen and over here at my farm. You need to come and get him." There was a pause, and then, "Yes, he wants honey." The voice rose higher. "Give him some? What? You know I love Pooh, but I'm very, very afraid he won't want to stop at just a taste."

All of this talk convinced Pooh. Somebody must've said 'Nobody,' and somebody had to be talking to somebody. Pooh didn't worry about all the other details. Everyone knew he loved honey, and he really did just want a little honey. He could stop eating. He always did stop eating-eventually. *Farmer, my nice friend, will give me some honey. I will eat it all and stop eating.* "Farmer, isn't that you? This voice I'm hearing sounds like my friend the farmer's voice."

As Pooh said that, he either leaned on the gate by accident or a playful gust of wind helped by pushing the gate open just a bit. An open gate was much different from a closed gate. Pooh wasn't supposed to go through closed gates, but an open gate was an invitation to enter. Pooh walked through.

This time, as the voice answered Pooh, it sounded more desperate. "No, I don't think so. It isn't meant to be."

Pooh had walked around a corner of the house, and he said to his friend, "Hello, Farmer." Pooh always forgot the farmer's name, and maybe, because he thought of Peter as a rabbit's name, but the farmer wasn't a rabbit. So, he called him 'Farmer.'

The farmer stood holding a tub marked in bold print with the words "fresh honey." He looked at Pooh and said, "Oh, hello, Pooh."

Then the farmer looked at him again and quickly moved the tub behind his back. Pooh didn't understand what the print on the tub meant, but his nose had told him there was honey in the tub.

His friend Farmer said, "Oh, Pooh. What a pleasant surprise."

Meanwhile, another voice from a pocket in his friend's jacket said, "You know how Pooh is with honey. Let him have some. We will

17

of course pay you. Tell him firmly that after he eats it, he must go home and wait for us at his pen. We have some berries for him."

There was a pause, and then slowly with careful enunciation the voice said, "Remember, be very careful what you tell Pooh. He takes things quite literally." The voice sounded like Pooh's human mother, but... how could that be? She wouldn't fit in a pocket. Pooh didn't understand.

His friend said, "Would you like some honey, Pooh?"

At those words, Pooh wanted to hug his friend, but fortunately, he remembered in time that hugging was similar to sitting on laps. "Oh, yes." Pooh remembered how his human family had taught him to be polite. "Thank you, Farmer."

With a big sigh, Farmer pointed to a shady area under a big tree. "Go sit under that tree. I'm going inside, and I'll be back. After you eat all of the honey, you need to go back home."

Pooh didn't quite understand everything, but at the idea of eating all of the honey, he hurried over to the shade and sat down. "Okay, I'm ready."

The little bear looked around. Where had Farmer gone? He said he would go inside. What had he gone inside of?

The question puzzled Pooh. He tried to remember just what he'd been told. The one phrase that had stuck came back to him. "After you eat all of the honey, you need to go back home."

Pooh looked around for the honey. He couldn't see any. Fortunately, his nose had been looking. His nose always did a better job of finding everything.

His nose told him where the honey waited for him.

Pooh stood up. Farmer hadn't told him to stay in the shade. *He told me to sit in the shade, and then eat all of the honey. I've already sat in the shade.* The little bear started walking. He followed his nose. His nose told him to keep going. Eventually, he heard a buzzing and more buzzing. Then, he saw white blocky shapes.

The closer Pooh got, the clearer he understood where the honey was. That was a lot of honey. For a moment, Pooh paused. What had Farmer said? Did he really say eat all of the honey? Pooh's stomach didn't like him pausing. His feet resumed moving forward. *That's funny. I didn't think of walking closer.* He considered again Farmer's words. Pooh had a suspicion, but he wanted the honey, and he didn't want Farmer to be mad, and Farmer had said to eat all of the honey before he went home.

With a sigh of pure joy and contentment, Pooh set to work. He didn't hear Farmer calling his name until it was too late. Other trouble Pooh had no idea about kept coming closer.

Chapter Three

Fuego

Hummingbirds are incredible creatures. Their wings beat from 12 to 80 beats per second. Their heart rate ranges from about 50 to 1,260 beats per minute. They react much faster than humans. Compared to a hummingbird, humans move like a sloth. That is amazing and crazy. They are the most colorful of birds, and many of their colors are in the ultraviolet range. Humans can't see all of their colors. Only other birds can. Hummingbirds see farther than humans and into the ultraviolet range.

Hummingbirds both make and hear ultrasonic noises that humans cannot hear. This is fairly new knowledge from 2024. There is so much we don't know about hummingbirds. Another thing we do know is male hummingbirds are very, very territorial. That means hummingbird males can have strong and aggressive attitudes. Also, they are curious and have a great memory.

Fuego couldn't stop flying. *I can't see the sky. I've got to get out of here. I don't want to lose control. Cooking one of my friends would be bad. They might not forgive me.* Fear and stress almost made Fuego not notice the clickety-clack background noise of the train. For the last while, the repeating noise was slower and the air seemed to be getting cooler. Fuego ignored the conversation of his friends. *Why have I decided to have friends? What am I doing in here? I've got to get out.*

He flew over to his portable hummingbird feeder. The drink wasn't sweet enough. Even as he drank the sugar water from the feeder, Fuego heard the tiger Tigger asking another question.

In an annoyed voice, Tigger asked, "Why are we stuck inside this cage?"

That question hit a very responsive nerve in the high-strung hummingbird and started his anger fuse burning.

The little cat, the little dog, and the raven slept through this part of the discussion. Noah the young man with them tried to answer. The little hummingbird recognized Noah's impatience in his voice. "I've already told you. We have a long way to go, and this is the easiest way to get there."

Noah added, "Fuego, do you have to keep buzzing back and forth?"

Fuego had had enough. *Noah was impatient? What? Noah had made this choice to travel in a box.* Fuego's normal rapid heartbeat increased to over twelve-hundred beats per second.

Tuffy the red-tailed hawk and the other one still awake, ruffled his feathers on his perch and asked, "But why did we decide to go, and what happened to the crystal? Have you forgotten that Star died in our effort to get that crystal?"

That question hit more nerves in Fuego. He flew back and forth, faster and faster.

Noah sighed and answered, "Remember? We all talked about it. All of you creatures can do special things. Down in southern Utah is a new place where you'll learn how to better use those special things. You need the training."

Fuego flew up and hovered in front of Noah's face. Quickly, he said, "Okay, I get that."

21

He continued, "You didn't answer about the crystal."

Getting irritated by the topic, Fuego spoke faster. "We fought and risked our lives to get that crystal. Don't you remember?"

At the emotion in the hummingbird's words, Noah ducked to the side. That turned out to be a good idea because at Fuego's next statement, a small ball of fire burst out in front of the bird before dying away with a poof right where Noah's head had been.

"That big man killed our friend Star." Fuego added, "Oops, sorry."

Everyone moved back from Fuego. The little bird zipped back and forth. "You're all still scared of me."

His words fired out of him. "Well, that's okay. It is good to be scared of me. I'm fierce and dangerous. So get used to it, but have I ever hurt any of you?"

"Noah jumping in front of my fireball doesn't count. The fireball died as it crisped a few hairs."

The little hummer dashed about, and everyone awake had retreated as far as they could in the confines of the boxcar.

Noah warned Tigger, "Don't make a hole in this boxcar to jump out."

Fuego didn't stop his complaints. "I saved everyone in that fight."

"I stopped the eagle from stealing that crystal. I did it, and here I am stuck in this box."

"Do we have the important crystal? What happened to the bad man? Did any of you ask me if I wanted to go to this Utah place? I don't need this training. I'm fine."

The little bird flew beak up to the tiger's nose and said, "Make a small hole in this trap. Then, you won't have to be frightened of me anymore."

Tigger said, "There, behind you."

Fuego turned. Dust from what had been part of the wall fell to the floor. The hummingbird flew out of the new hole. Immediately, the wind caught him, but instantly, the little hummingbird reacted to the wind and flew away from the train and toward the trees.

The hummingbird looked around, taking in the evergreens. These trees were different from the ones he knew. He heard an alarm call from a little bird. His sharp eyes caught the yellows, reds, and ultraviolet colors of flowers.

The little bird sounding the alarm said, "Hawk, flying overheard, danger, danger."

A sharp shinned hawk dove to kill Fuego.

Fuego didn't know it was a sharp shinned hawk, but he recognized the hawk's intent. Fuego'd been chased before. He blasted from about fifteen miles per hour to thirty five miles per hour.

He left the hawk behind and for full measure darted around a tree and—

Another hawk almost exactly like the first crashed through some branches to get at him. In fifty heartbeats, Fuego both thought '*That had to hurt.*' and dove into a canyon. Down the canyon he went following a small stream bed below him.

Fuego sizzled around a big clump of trees and darted down to a tight thicket with large branches. He decided to enter from the back of the thicket. *This will give me safety even if they managed to follow me.*

Moving from bright sunlight into shadows, Fuego hovered behind a large tree. *Spiderwebs.* Some of them caught his wings. A spider moved toward him from a nearby branch. Fortunately for

Fuego, this spider was not as big or as fast as his southern relative the golden orb spider. Fuego was only three inches long. That southern one might've killed Fuego, just like it had killed other hummingbirds.

At the sight of the spider moving toward him, terror pulsed through the tiny bird's body. Small spiders tasted good, but this one was entirely too big. *I'm stuck. It'll get me.*

A fireball burst from Fuego incinerating the nearby spider webs, the spider, and catching some of the dry branches on fire.

A chattering, scolding voice rose from another part of the tree. "Fire! Fire! What are you doing?"

A chipmunk raced toward Fuego and the growing fire. "You're going to burn down my tree and this forest, you idiot."

A fog enveloped the fire. The smoke and fog cleared revealing the blackened remains of the brief fire, but the scolding continued. "Got scared by a spider? Stupid, that spider didn't threaten you. You almost burned down the forest."

Fuego shivered and backed up. Another fog cloud had enveloped him, leaving him cold. "What did you do?"

In a smug voice, the chipmunk answered, "I made you cold. Unfortunately, I can't freeze predators, but I can make life hard on them. They've mostly learned to leave me alone. You need to learn to control your use of fire. I also use heat to make seeds easier to eat. They're tastier too."

In the chaos of the spider web, the fire and then the crazy chipmunk, Fuego had almost forgotten about the hawks. He twirled, looking for the bigger predators. They seemed to have given up.

Fuego looked back at the chipmunk. "Hey, I'm sorry about the fire. I'm trying to get it under control." *Noah tried to convince me to get the training.*

24

"You need to practice, to train with it. I don't want you burning down my forest. Fires are bad. I've practiced with my abilities."

The chipmunk kept moving and talking. "I like the results of my training. I used to talk too much, but I've worked at it. I don't talk nearly as much. Hey, I can heat up a pinecone until it pops releasing its seeds. Want to see. Come on. It's easier than chewing it."

The hyper little chipmunk didn't wait for a response. It scampered head first down the tree trunk and jumped to the ground. "This is a great trick. Nobody else can do this, but watch me."

Curious, the little hummingbird followed. Fuego still looked for the hawks or other predators. This was a new place. He didn't know what might be dangerous. The chipmunk had been right. The spider had been too small to threaten Fuego. *Training, that's right. That was what Noah wanted to help me with.* The little bird didn't want to agree with the idea even in his own thoughts. *What will I do now? Having friends had been nice. They weren't always stupid.*

The little chipmunk scampered, jumped, and bounced over the ground. Fuego found watching the little creature to be fascinating. The chipmunk found a pinecone and rolled it into an open spot. At first, nothing seemed to be happening. With an audible pop, the pinecone scales opened.

The hawks. Fuego screamed a warning. "Hawks, run!"

Fuego buzzed toward the thicket. Almost instantly, he saw the chipmunk wouldn't make it to safety.

The hummingbird reversed course. He flew back at the hawks. Fuego screamed a challenge. "Leave him alone."

The two hawks had almost no time to change course. A fireball blazed at the one almost getting the chipmunk. The bird twisted away from attacking.

The chipmunk made it to safety. "Leave us alone or you'll regret it." A ball of fog appeared around the other hawk.

It flew out covered in ice. The hawks landed in a nearby tree and watched them. "We'll get you for this."

The little chipmunk said, "Ha, I don't think so. I've got friends."

Voices of other animals in the woods started screaming insults at the two hawks.

Fuego flew into the thicket and landed. He waited. His heart rate slowly subsided. *Friends. He has friends. Why was I such an idiot?*

The chipmunk dashed up a trunk near Fuego. "Thanks for the help. You did good. Kept your fire from trees."

"Thanks. If you want to go back and get some more seeds, I can keep a watch for danger."

"No, it's getting late. How about if we rest near each other? It will be safer tonight."

"Okay, but first, I'm going back out. There are a couple of good blooms nearby. I'll be right back."

The time flew past as Fuego darted about. He hovered momentarily, at each bloom. At a particularly sweet smell, he changed course to a tall purple flower. The nectar in its blooms finished filling him up. Just under thirty-five seconds later, Fuego returned.

The chipmunk scolded from down by the ground. "I almost gave up waiting for you. Follow me. Hurry."

Hurry? Fuego made a point of following very closely behind the crazy chipmunk. The small creature scurried through the forest to a large old pine tree. Racing up the trunk, the chipmunk slipped into a small hole.

For a moment, Fuego paused just outside the hole. He noticed a shadowy form silently flying down from the darkening sky. The owl made the decision for the hummingbird. Fuego followed the chipmunk into the hole. Inside, he just had enough room to hover.

The chipmunk had already curled up and seemed to be falling asleep. Fuego found a crevice in the cavity. He squeezed in and quickly started falling into his nighttime torpor.

Fuego's heartbeats slowed. At times, his breathing stopped. The noises of the chipmunk slowly pulled him back to awareness.

"Wow, you sleep soundly. Good thing I'm trustworthy. I could've easily eaten you. Not that I would've. I might've eaten an egg or two in my lifetime. I can't stand this waiting. Bye. See you later."

Finally, cautiously, Fuego exited the cavity. *Why did I trust that chipmunk?* Fuego knew the answer. The chipmunk had been a bit crazy, easy to get upset, not very patient, with a short attention span, and he reminded the little hummingbird of himself. Fuego hovered just outside the hole. He looked around. Already, the chipmunk was nowhere to be seen.

Last evening, Fuego had seen some promising flowers and they smelled sweet. A few darting sips and Fuego had refueled. He hovered carefully, watching his surroundings as something strange caught his attention.

Fuego zoomed up. Something flew high above the trees. At first, he couldn't make any sense of it. The object didn't look like any bird. *It's really moving fast.*

The approaching thing flew faster than Fuego could. In shock at his recognition of the object, he almost stopped flying. It's a big black dog flying through the air.

What's going on? Flying beside the dog... *That's Izzy.*

I like her. She speaks her mind. Maybe, she's going to join Noah. I sure would like to give him a piece of my mind. What was he thinking letting me leave? I need that training.

Fuego had always liked the dark-skinned, teenage woman. He angled his flight to try and intersect their course. Before he could get high enough, the strange dog and Izzy streaked past.

Fuego picked up his speed and gave chase. The pair continued flying in a straight line. Soon, they would be over the tallest mountain in the area. *At the speed they're going, they'll be almost out of sight by the time I reach that mountain.*

He flew at his maximum level flight speed, but they were going more than twice his speed. Fuego didn't want to give up the chase. *I'm fueled up. I can keep this up all morning. They have to land eventually. I can fly longer than they can.*

Just before he reached the mountain, a jet roared past. It maneuvered in front of the pair. At their distance from Fuego, he couldn't be sure, but it looked a little like the aerial combat he'd had with yellow jackets. Mesmerized, Fuego watched as he flew past the crest of the mountain.

I'm getting close. Fuego couldn't keep his max speed up for much longer. Fuego had more fuel in his tank, but he was getting tired and cold. If I could get close enough, I can help them with my fire. In the far distance and higher, Fuego spotted another jet much higher coming toward them. As if that wasn't bad enough, there were some helicopters coming from a different direction.

The jet swerved in even closer to the flying dog and Izzy. Fuego saw something tumble.

Chapter Four

Annie and Izzy

PTSD (Post traumatic stress disorder) is not just something those with war experiences deal with. Any traumatic event can cause it. PTSD may start soon after the event or not until years later. It can result in negative changes in thinking and mood. In this story, Izzy has to deal with fears as a result of her PTSD.

As sometimes happens in times of fear and disruption, things change quickly and not necessarily for the better. Often, people or organizations cause those things to happen. Fear and disruption have always been used as a source of power.

After helping her friends get the crystal, Izzy had worked at getting her business ready for reopening. The repairs had been easier than she'd expected. Izzy laughed at the memory of how the tiger had looked flipping through the air right before he popped her bounce house. Immediately after the brief laugh, Izzy snorted. It really hadn't seemed very funny at the time. She'd been furious.

The more Izzy thought of the past, the more part of her wanted to be irritated. She tried to shove the irritation away. *It wasn't that bad, and I'm almost done getting ready to reopen.* The slender, athletic, young black woman brushed a strand of her beautiful frizzy hair out of her face. Izzy glanced at the ladder with the big bucket of water precariously perched near the top. *I really need to finish washing the windows in front of my business.* Izzy'd started that job, but nervousness at being so high had made her stop twice already.

The afternoon sunlight shining through the windows showed which windows still needed cleaning. Streaks on some windowpanes testified to how much soap she'd used.

Izzy remembered how she'd already done one of the more terrifying jobs. Izzy looked at the ladder leading to the catwalk. She'd gone up there and out the door in the ceiling and onto the roof.

The effort at recalling the success had been meant to encourage herself, but instead, all she thought of was the terror of each step and the effort it had taken.

Izzy walked toward the ladder by the window in resignation. She hated her fear of going back up that ladder. Part of her, an illogical part, wanted to knock the ladder over. That, of course, would be stupid. She grinned at the idea of the bucket of very soapy water landing on someone else's head. She was thinking of her friend who had helped cause some of the damage. Even though she tried to let it go and truly forgive him, she still remembered how mad it had made her. Breathing deep, she pushed away the residual anger and her unreasonable fear of heights. *I can do this.*

Through the windows, Izzy saw two people approaching her front door. *Who would that be?* The size of the much larger individual seemed familiar. A knock at the front doors interrupted her thoughts. The smaller of them had knocked. Hurrying to answer, Izzy didn't think to worry about who it would be. The guards at the deli would keep away anyone dangerous.

Before she could reach the doors, trucks pulled up, and men jumped out of them. She paused in surprise.

The big man opened the door and stepped in. He wore a little hat perched on his very large head. The hat had the letters NGO on it. At the sight, Izzy's blood ran cold, her stomach clenched, and a shiver ran down her back.

The smaller woman followed him into Izzy's business. The big man stepped farther in, forcing Izzy to back up. He bumped the ladder. A squeak came from the floor, as the legs of the ladder scraped against her clean concrete floor.

Startled, Izzy glanced up at the bucket even as she backed up more and gawked at the man. She recognized him. He was the big boss who they had caught as they raced to secure an important crystal before he could get it. *What is he doing here? Why is he free? He should be locked up somewhere.* Seeing the big man and her terror of him being free brought back a much older and even more horrible memory.

Another big, terrible man had broken into her home when Izzy had been just a little girl. He had threatened all of them and had hit her dad with his gun. For months, Izzy'd been terrified of anyone new, hadn't been able to sleep, and had been frightened all the time.

A cold sweat broke out on her forehead. In a little girl's voice, Izzy told herself, *I can deal with this.*

The second individual surprised her as well. Izzy knew the small woman as a government secret agent who Noah had met. What was she doing with this terrible man?

The horrible and very nasty man said, "Surprised to see me?" He gave an evil laugh. "My Non-Governmental Organization,"—he pointed to his hat that said NGO on it—"has a contract with the government to research what's going on. We're going to find out how some creatures can now play with laws of physics. We're getting very close to some important results. There's one animal in particular, and I have decided your building will work quite nicely."

He added in a very calm manner, "Oops, that is classified information. I'm afraid you don't have clearance to know it. Anyone without clearance will be killed if they find out." He grinned.

Stubbornly, Izzy ignored the terror his words tried to ignite. Izzy hated how her hands shook at his words and propped them on her hips. With her elbows jutting out, Izzy said, in the firmest voice she could manage, "You can't do that."

Men had already propped the doors open, and others carried boxes through the entrance. Izzy noticed two very strange-looking individuals amongst all the men. One had hair spiked a foot into the air. The hair was bright orange with dull olive-green stripes.

Izzy couldn't tell if it was a man or a woman. That one wore heavy, black boots laced halfway up its shins. Metal piercings covered its body and very little clothing hid the metal. A shiny metal chain hung from the person's waist and a number of other metal objects hung from it. The person bumped carelessly against the ladder.

Izzy quickly looked up at the bucket. It wobbled but didn't fall.

The second one's hair looked moldy. Its hair hung straight down to its waist. The hair colors were a dark mildewy-green with light purplish-pink stripes. The shorts and small top it had on revealed tattoos covering most of its body. With a start, Izzy realized the tattoos moved and changed. Izzy felt sick.

Even the person's clothing looked moldy, and the person had on strange-looking shoes. Izzy couldn't tell how its feet could fit in the shoes. The heels had to be at least a foot high.

The second one stopped in front of Izzy and looked her up and down. "You're strange. What weird, kinky hair you have. You should get it straightened."

Izzy opened her mouth to respond even as her mind struggled with what to say. The worst of it was the moldy one had made her feel strange. *I am not strange. How did she do that? My kinky hair is great.*

The other, the first one, turned back. "She is strange, but we have a job to do. Be careful not to trip. This floor is a mess."

32

Izzy looked at her floor. *My floor is clean, and—* The men were leaving boxes everywhere. Now, men brought cages filled with assorted animals. From those cages smelly, stinky stuff fell onto the floor. Men stepped in it with a squish and tracked it all over.

Four men carried a big cage through the entrance. It held a huge, beautiful, black dog. Izzy recognized the breed. It was a female Newfie.

The dog stared back at Izzy and said in a low rumbly voice, "Could we be friends?"

One of the men said, "Let's put this heavy thing down over here."

Before they could put it down, another man said, "Look out."

The two strange people faced each other talking as they walked back, and they ran into the side of the cage. They fell, taking one of the men down with them.

Izzy expected the cage would crash onto the floor too, and it started to, but it stopped and lifted back up.

One of the men said, "Thanks, mutt."

From behind Izzy, she heard the fat man say, "Careful with that mutt. We are getting very close to success with that one."

Izzy whirled around, and stared at the huge man. Again, she protested, "This is my business. You can't do this."

The agent, or whatever she was, just looked at Izzy with a neutral expression.

At first, the fat man ignored Izzy. "Be careful with that dog. Anyone who hurts that dog will be very, very sorry."

The horrible man's concern for an animal surprised Izzy. *What's so important about this dog? He hates animals.* "You can't get away with threatening people."

33

The man continued, "From the preliminary experimental results, I think that dog is going to unlock how to control gravity. We are going to run some more tests and finish building the world's first gravity machine."

The big horrid man looked at Izzy with an evil smile. He waved his hand at the activity. "In case you haven't noticed, I am doing what I want to do. Soon, I will have incredible powers. I just need a little more time with that mutt." He laughed again. "Have you noticed how unworried I am about you learning what I am doing? Soon, I will stop having to see your ugly, black, frizzy hair."

Izzy had had it. They couldn't just come in here, ruin everything, threaten her like this, insult her looks, and just take her business. *I'll go get the guards from the deli. They know me. They'll help me.*

As her luck would have it, at that moment one of the guards walked through the door. Izzy recognized her. She was Elliana. The guard carefully stepped around the ladder with its bucket of soapy water perched on it.

Izzy grinned. A wave of relief swept through her. Now, this man and his henchmen would get what was coming to them. Izzy knew and trusted the guards. They were all her friends. She had told them about how terrible this fat man was.

Elliana had an odd expression on her face. She looked at Izzy. *Are those tears in her eyes?* The way her face looked wasn't what Izzy had expected. Elliana turned to the fat man and said, "I have been forced to check on you and offer any help you might need."

Izzy wanted to find somewhere to hide and cry, but at those words, something inside Izzy broke. *How could Elliana do this? How could she let herself be forced to do what was obviously wrong? What has happened? This can't be.*

Rebellion and rage ignited in her heart. She didn't know what she would do, but one thing she did know. She wasn't going to let this happen without a fight.

Izzy clenched her hands into fists. She wouldn't live her life in fear. She wouldn't let this man hurt her.

The fat man backed away from her. Izzy tried to follow, but an iron grip on her arm stopped her. The shorter, small lady held her by the arm and whispered, "Come with me."

Louder, the small lady said, "I'll have a talk with her and get the layout of her business. Then, you can do what you want with her."

She started dragging Izzy away from the evil man. At that moment, the two strange people came in carrying a pole. One went under the ladder, but the other didn't. A man yelled, "Stop!"

They didn't stop. The ladder tipped over with a crash. The bucket of water landed upside down on the fat man's head. The two staggered about with the pole and hit the bucket on the man's head once, twice, three times, and then he fell down. Three men ran over to help him, but they slipped on the soapy floor and landed on top of him.

Quiet laughter from the small lady surprised Izzy. Izzy had laughed out loud at the wonderful disaster.

The lady quietly said, in humor accented words, "We've got to get back to your office before I laugh out loud."

Izzy stopped fighting against the agent and let the woman lead her back to her office. Once they were through the door, Izzy started to ask a question, "What's—"

The lady firmly placed a hand over Izzy's mouth and whispered, "shhh." Louder, she added, "I don't care about your feelings. You're going to cooperate with me or else." Then, she slammed the door of the office behind them.

Through the wall came yells. It didn't sound like things were getting better out there. Izzy grinned in fierce pleasure at the image of the soapy mess they'd left behind.

The agent took her hand away. Quickly and quietly, the lady added, "The back door and front door are being guarded. Do you know another way out of here?"

Izzy shivered at the idea of the other way. "There's a door onto the roof."

"Perfect. You've got to get out of here. You can use Annie to get away. In fact, you need to protect Annie and get her to Noah."

Izzy looked at the office door, struggling with the ideas. *How can I get away from the roof? Who's Annie? How can I use Annie to escape? Take her to Noah?* That last had a great sound to it.

The agent continued talking, "Take this. It's a map showing where Noah and the animals are going. The animals are going to get some training from a specialist. It would be good for Annie. Once you get there, you'll be safe."

Izzy felt her press something else into the palm of her hand. "This is a key to all of the cages. Free Annie and use her to escape. Just ask Annie, and she'll be happy to help you. I'll make a distraction. Be careful on your journey. This horrible NGO has at least some jets and other military units."

Get Annie. Go out through the roof. Escape? How would she escape with Annie? Protect Annie? "Who's Annie?"

"She's that huge dog. She's a sweetie. You using her to get away will be wonderful. It will save her from being experimented on. They are close to a powerful breakthrough. I hate what this man is doing, but his NGO has too much power. They got him out of his trouble. The government is frightened, and this NGO is telling them they can help. Once they gain control of gravity, I doubt they'll be helping the government or listening to the government. I think they plan on being the new government."

36

Izzy remembered the dog and its cage not falling, but actually lifting up. *The dog did that?* "What can that dog do?" *How could she—*

"Annie can take you to Noah. She can control gravity."

Automatically, Izzy asked, "How can a dog take me to Noah?" The rest of what the agent had said hit Izzy. *Gravity? That dog can control gravity?* In her shock, Izzy hardly listened to the rest of what the agent had said or what she continued saying.

"Getting Annie to Noah is very important, but this is also important information. The crystal was taken back east. Some politicians wanted to see it. One of my fellow agents is guarding it. I recommended giving it back to Noah. Your friend's a genius. If anyone can figure it out, Noah can. Hopefully, my fellow agent will get it back to Noah, but I know this idiot's boss down in Utah wants it. All I know about the man is he's down by the place Noah is going. If the NGO gains control of it, they might bring it here."

She handed Izzy a small flat device. "Hold this flat and push the button in the middle. I have a tracker on Noah. This device will help you find him. There are vast areas of mountains south of us and some wilderness areas, but you must be careful. I've heard reports there are even higher numbers of animals doing unusual things there. Because of that, they are very dangerous. Try to avoid spending any time in them."

The lady kept talking. "If the crystal is returned here, I'll get it. If it is taken to this idiot's boss, you, Noah, and the animals will need to get it back. Meanwhile, I'm trying to get enough information to put this guy's boss in prison for a very long time. I need to shut down this NGO before they get more power. The things it has done are horrible, and they are planning much worse things."

The agent walked over to a cabinet and started fiddling with the door.

Izzy said, "I haven't been able to open that cabinet for—" She stopped talking and just gazed in shock as the agent opened the door and retrieved a package. Izzy just managed one word. "What?"

The agent said, "I had these delivered here last night. The person doing the delivery had a terrible time with this cabinet, but it made a great place to hide these."

"What are they?"

"You've heard about how dark matter has affected some huckleberries?"

Izzy went from shock to shock. At the mention of the berries, she recognized the smell coming from the package. At first, all Izzy could do was point at the package and say, "Huckleberries?" She stepped back.

The little lady ruefully grinned. "Yeah, you've heard about them. At least they still taste great."

Over their conversation, the yells had continued. They still sounded mad, but there was less chaos. Izzy wished that the bucket had been bigger and even soapier.

The agent pulled two pills from a pocket. "Take one of these and get the dog to take the other. Just stick it way back into her mouth, and Annie will swallow it. At least, that's what the vet told me."

Izzy shuddered at the idea of huckleberries. Reluctantly, she took the pills. Izzy had loved the fruit in the past, but now... "What about you?"

"I'll just have to suffer along with everyone else. I can't appear to know about the berries. The amnesia the berries cause will mean it doesn't matter what I do or say before I dump the berries. While the rest of us are going crazy, you get Annie and go out the roof door and leave. Go south. Find Noah and the others. Most importantly, get Annie to Noah, and, if you can, help protect the crystal."

At those words, Izzy felt her heart drop into one of her feet. Which one, she wasn't sure. Realistically, she knew that hadn't happened, but it felt like it. Izzy wanted to voice her objections to the idea, but she didn't get a chance. The only thing she did manage to do was to grab her backpack.

The agent grabbed Izzy by the arm and tugged her back toward the door. "Now, go get Annie to swallow the pill. I can't spill the berries until you've done that. It wouldn't do to have her go crazy."

The door opened in front of Izzy, and a purple soap bubble floated peacefully into the office. More soap bubbles floated gently around.

Various piles of people struggled to get untangled in the soapy mess. Other people crawled on the slippery floor, only to fall flat on the floor, giving voice to their anger.

The big boss had managed to get to the edge of the soap mess. *He's between me and Annie.* He pointed at her. "What's she doing loose? I want her in a cage or dead. Preferably in a cage, so we can run experiments on her."

Chapter Five

Pooh's Great Adventure Begins

Trees can be connected by their root systems, and thus they can form a superorganism. Even stumps can be kept alive. Trees and other plants also respond to light by growing toward light. They respond to external stimuli and share chemical messages between each other.

Winnie the Pooh had adventures with his friends. I just had an adventure, but it made my friends mad. Pooh cried at that thought. A small bump jostled him. If only, he hadn't gotten into such trouble. Pooh still remembered his stomach ache. He shouldn't have eaten so much, but Farmer had said to eat it all. The truck went around a corner, and Pooh leaned. It was all too confusing for Pooh. How was it big trouble if his foster father laughed about it?

Pooh squirmed at the memory of Farmer's reaction. He remembered his foster mother had cried. It must've been big trouble. He thought. *Why couldn't I understand and stay out of trouble? What am I going to do now?* Pooh scratched his head. *I need to think harder about how to stay out of trouble.* The truck he rode in went over a bad bump shaking him out of his own thoughts.

The little bear looked through the window into the cab at the driver his human father. Pooh didn't remember his bear mother. She had died when he was very young. The only family he'd known was this man and his wife. They had raised him and taught him everything he knew.

His father pointed at the lake and said, "Pooh, look at the fish."

Pooh looked and saw balls of water floating through the air. Bright red fish swam in those balls. A big bird dived at one of them, but the ball and the fish dodged it. *Wow. That's so cool.*

His father said, "Those fish are doing something crazy with gravity."

The little bear scratched his head in confusion. *Gravity holds us down. How can fish do anything with gravity? Gravity didn't hold those fish down.* Pooh looked at one of the fish in its bubble. *That fish and the water shouldn't be floating.* As if in response to his thoughts, the ball of water disintegrated into just water falling through the air. At first, the fish fell until it seemed to dive more gracefully back into the lake.

His dad said, "This area by the lake is dangerous. We won't stop."

Pooh puzzled over the gravity question, as they drove to the end of the road. The thinking made his head hurt.

His dad stopped the truck and got out. "Okay, Pooh." He pointed over to a sign. "This is where we start hiking to your new home."

"Do I have to? I'm sorry I made our friend Farmer mad. I apologized."

His dad looked at Pooh standing in the bed of the truck and sighed. "Pooh, you are no longer just a little bear. You need to take what we've taught you and live in the wild."

Dejectedly, Pooh gave up. They'd already had this talk three times on the way from their home. He climbed down out of the truck.

His dad pointed at the overgrown trail and the mountains above them. Tall, straight trees grew on either side of the path. "Pooh, humans used to come up here all the time. In these mountains, you are going to become the big powerful bear you are meant to be. You are one of those new young animals that can do very special things. Remember what we've taught you."

Pooh listened before following. *I can't do those special things Dad has talked about except for smelling. My nose is special.*

Together, they began the hike. The smell of water came from somewhere ahead and off the trail. Pooh wandered a little way off the trail and looked down at a stream bed. The little bear glimpsed a slender animal sliding past. *That looks fun. It's playing.* The animal had a musky smell. Pooh started to turn away, but another smell caught his attention. He smelled a bear.

The little bear wanted to climb down to the stream and find the bear. He took the first step down, but his dad's voice called him back. He noticed another smell, dog-like but stronger.

"Come on, Pooh."

Pooh turned and ran up the steadily rising trail. The air smelled different. A tasty looking plant caught his attention. Munching on it, Pooh looked back at his dad.

Pooh's dad gazed back down the glacial valley. "I understand your sadness at leaving our home, but you need to live in the wild. There, you will make your own story." He waved his hand at the valley and beautiful lake below them. "This valley and Lake Wallowa are very important to my tribe's story. Now, the area around the lake is deserted except some say a dangerous person lives in the old lodge." His dad looked thoughtful and said, "I was surprised that there wasn't more wildlife around the lake. I wonder what is going on, but you won't have to worry about it."

Pooh walked closer and looked, but he couldn't see the lake clearly. He did remember the drive past it. *Did I see any other animals? My own story?* "Will my story be like the story of the other Pooh?"

His dad looked at him with a puzzled expression. "The other Pooh? Ooh, you mean Winnie the Pooh of the story."

"Yes."

"Pooh, that was a make-believe story. Yours will be different."

The little bear sat down. "I want to be part of your story."

His father sat cross-legged on the ground by him. "Pooh, we can't always do what we want. My tribe wanted their story to continue in this valley, but they were forced to leave. We had to make a new story."

"But why did your tribe let itself be forced to leave?"

"Pooh, they didn't want to leave. Other people came, like an ancestor of our friend Farmer. This and other things caused trouble. The government decided to solve it by taking our land and giving it to those people. My people went on a journey over a thousand miles long trying to avoid being forced to do what they didn't want. Our horses, like the ones next to our home, were a big part of that journey."

The little bear scratched his head. "Why did they go on a journey? You said they didn't want to leave, but then they went on a journey."

For a long moment, his dad just looked at him. Pooh patiently waited. A different expression crossed his father's face. The little bear didn't know what the expression meant.

"Pooh, you are a wonderful, loving, and simple bear. I've been going about this explanation the wrong way. The simple truth is you are going to keep getting bigger. You need to go. My wife and I can't take care of a big bear. We are very sad to say goodbye to you. Even our neighbor is going to be sad. Everyone loves you."

The little bear tried to understand. *If everyone is sad at my leaving, I shouldn't be leaving. Yet, Dad says I need to go. I don't understand.* A bird flew past. Pooh looked up at it. He grinned and pointed. "Look, Dad, a mountain bluebird. I remember your people believe a bluebird means a new beginning and good luck. Everything's going to be fine."

His dad grinned. "Pooh, it's hard to be sad with you around. Thank you for pointing out the bluebird. Remember, I also taught you that my tribe had many superstitions. When you start your new story, take the good and useful of the old, but always remember to be willing and ready to learn."

Pooh bounced up from the ground. "Let's get going, Dad. I can't wait to see how my new story's going to work out. Maybe I'll be a hero who saves everyone."

His dad said, "Pooh, stop. Look over there."

Pooh looked where his dad pointed. Back in the trees, he saw movement. At that distance and in the mottled shadows under the trees, Pooh had trouble making out what it was. He lifted his nose and smelled. "Is it a deer?"

"Yes. There are two of them."

The little bear moved from the trail. *Maybe they could be friends.*

"Wait. One of them is young."

I'm young. Maybe it can be my friend. Pooh continued moving closer.

In a sharper voice, his dad said, "Pooh, stop. You're forgetting that black bears eat deer."

"But I don't want to eat them. I want to be friends."

"Pooh, they don't know that. They'll think you're a threat. Many of the young deer in this area can play with physics. You're in danger.

44

Move back."

Physics? What's that? Pooh stopped. He could see the deer clearly now. They looked steadily back at him. He smelled again. There was that dog-like odor again.

Suddenly, they jumped, kicked, and, moving faster than he expected, ran away.

Pooh looked after them. *How did they move so fast? Would they have tried to hurt me? If I had been closer, I wouldn't have been able to dodge those kicks. I should've tried to talk with them.* The bear looked at his left front paw and waved it through the air. It flashed quickly through the air. The little bear didn't realize what he'd just done was unusual.

"That moving fast was their special thing. You need to be careful of other's abilities. Come on, Pooh. We need to keep going."

Pooh shrugged. He considered what had happened. *I wish I could think faster, but Dad has confidence in me.* The little bear turned back and hurried up the trail. Pooh could see the first part of the trail down below them. He smelled water down below them at the next bend in the trail. Again, Pooh smelled the musky smell of the slender animal he'd seen playing and a dog-like smell. *What are those other animals?*

Many things slowed him down. Pooh stopped to look at a beetle before he ate it. He leaned over to look at a single small, round blue berry. He knew it from his lessons. It was a queen's cup bead lily. It was very small, but Pooh opened his mouth. Just before he ate it, he remembered how much his mom loved seeing them. *I'll leave this. Others might hike along here and enjoy seeing it.*

Sunlight cut bars of light between the trees. Motes of dust drifted, and occasionally, insects flew through the bars of light.

A butterfly landed on his nose. Pooh looked at it, but it made his eyes hurt. The little bear shook the butterfly off and chased after it.

45

The insect flew up between some leaning tree trunks. Pooh climbed one of the trunks to where it joined, twenty feet up, with a half-dozen more trunks. From below, he heard his father.

"Wow. This is strange. I've never seen trees growing together like this."

Pooh looked at the trunks and the bigger one rising from the union. "They're a family making something bigger and stronger."

His dad said, "I think this is one of those new things, like fish being able to make bubbles of water float."

Pooh slid down the trunk to the ground. "Am I going to be able to float?"

The little bear ran and hopped over the ground. *This is a good adventure.*

His dad said, "Silly old bear, you're going the wrong direction."

Pooh tried to stop, and he succeeded, but by tumbling to a rather ungraceful, face down plop. He lifted his head up. "Why do you keep calling me old?"

"Because you are a silly old bear." His dad laughed.

Pooh got up and scratched his head. "It doesn't make any sense to me, but if it makes you laugh, it must be good. Let's go."

The little bear ran back to the trail and charged along. He didn't go far before he heard his dad calling after him to slow down. Pooh liked that idea. There were many tasty-looking plants, and he'd reached a part of the slope where cold air flowed down from big rocks above him. *This is a pleasant place.*

Pooh wandered off the trail to eat the juiciest plants. Another odd smell tickled his nose. *Something smelled like a rabbit or a mouse.*

A whistly voice interrupted Pooh's browsing. "What are you doing eating my food?"

The little bear looked up just in time to see a very small creature. It looked like a mixture of a rabbit and a mouse. "What are you?"

"I'm a pika, and if you don't leave my food alone, you'll be sorry."

Pooh didn't mean to keep eating. He was a very gentle soul. Pooh preferred to avoid trouble. Unfortunately, his mouth kept biting.

The next thing Pooh knew, something hit him in the side and knocked him head over tail. The little bear came to a stop back on the trail. Pooh thought he heard something like laughter back in the woods.

His father ran up to him. "Pooh, what happened?"

"Oh, nothing too much. I just wouldn't advise eating any plants around here."

"What?"

The little creature ran up to the edge of the trail. "This is my territory."

Pooh said, "He's a pika." And to the pika, Pooh said, "I'm sorry. I won't eat any more of your food. Would you like to play a game of Pooh ball?"

Pooh ball consisted of one person throwing a pinecone. The others then tried to lob a pinecone the closest to the first one. You had to throw the second pinecone underhand.

Pooh's dad and the pika spoke at the same time. "I don't think the pika can lob or throw a pinecone."

"A game? You're crazy. This is the haying season. I'm far too busy for a game. Get out of here. Leave me alone."

Pooh said, "We could help you."

"Help me? Can you tell which plants have the highest calories, protein, water, and most importantly, that are rich in phenolic compounds?"

The pika had dropped a mouthful of forbs. Pooh waved a paw at the tiny pile. He said, "Green plant stems just like those."

"You're too big and clumsy. You're wasting my important haying time."

"Come on, Pooh. We should get going." Pooh's dad resumed hiking up the trail.

Pooh looked hard at the small pile of forbs and a few grass stems. *I really would like to help him.* He looked to either side of the trail. He identified the right plants easily. *All I would have to do is to snap them off and pile them up.* Following his thoughts, a wave of something rippled through the area. The plants snapped off, lifted up, and drifted back through the air to pile up by the pika. Pooh said "Bye. I've got to go."

The little bear didn't think of what he'd done. Pooh hadn't realized that he'd done something unusual. He did feel a warm glow in his chest. It felt good to help others. Pooh hurried after his dad.

Huffing and puffing, Pooh ran up to his father before slowing down to walk behind him.

"Pooh, what you offered back there was very nice. Being nice in the wild can be bad. Remember, up here in the wild, other animals aren't going to be nice. Wolves will try to eat you. You'll have to defend yourself. That little pika back there and marmots are potential food for you. Most of the time, you can't be nice. Remember at home the meat you ate? That came from dead animals. Be cautious about helping others."

The little bear followed without saying anything. *I can't be nice?*

48

His thoughts went back to the story Pooh. *That bear had friends. They were nice to each other. I don't want this story my dad is telling me about. I want friends. You have friends by being nice.*

Wordlessly, the father and bear continued up the trail. Pooh noticed the dog-like smell grow stronger. *I should tell Dad something is following us.* At the sight of a small dam and a quiet pond the thought dropped from Pooh's mind. At the sight of the water, Pooh rushed over to drink the cool, refreshing water.

In the middle of his drinking, a voice interrupted. "Hello. What do we have here? What's a bear doing with a human? And what's a human doing up here?"

Pooh looked up. On the other side of the pond, a coyote looked back at them. Pooh lifted his nose and smelled. *A dog-like smell. This is what I smelled earlier.*

"Hello, Coyote. This is my adopted son. His mother died, and my wife and I have raised Pooh. I'm taking him up to Lake Aneroid. That should be a good place for him to start living by himself in the wild."

The coyote said, "Hmmm, it's dangerous for a human to go up there. I'll take your bear-son to the lake. I know the way. That whole area is good for bears."

Pooh's dad said, "Why should I trust you? Coyotes are known as tricksters."

"True. We can come up with fun things, but if you are worried about your son, why are you planning on leaving him alone?"

A long pause filled the air with silence broken only by the burbling of the stream flowing into the pond. Pooh interrupted the quiet. "Would you be my friend?" *With a friend, I could enjoy my new story.*

The coyote shifted and tilted his head. "Well, of course I can be your friend. Did you know there are wolves up here?" At the word 'wolves,' the coyote looked back over his shoulder before continuing. "They don't like me. By traveling with you and you with me, we'd both be safer. They would love to eat a young bear like you. What do you say, friend?"

Chapter Six

Takeoff

Gravity is one of the most interesting physical forces. In one sense, it is very simple. Objects with more mass have more gravity. The farther from an object, the less you feel its gravity. These things we know, but we do not know how gravitational force is transmitted. Some theories postulate a hypothetical particle called the graviton. That particle transmits gravity. In Einstein's theory, gravity isn't transmitted, but is rather a consequence of the curvature of space time caused by mass and energy. That is mind stretching stuff, and here is more and very exciting mind stretching stuff. Imagine what you could do if you could control gravity.

Being able to control gravity would be a game changer. How would you like to fly through the air? The ability to control gravity would affect all of life. Moving things would become much, much easier. Unfortunately, controlling gravity would probably get used in some way as a weapon. Very powerful people would do anything to gain that power.

The two strange people looked at Izzy. "Okay, Boss. We'll take care of her."

He hollered at them. "Help me out of here first." He had managed to get up on all fours.

The two strange people still had the pole. Staying well away from the soap, they carefully poked it toward the boss.

The boss reached for the pole, but he missed it and almost fell flat onto the soapy floor. He yelled at them. "It's too far away. Either come over here and just pull me out of this or jab the stupid pole over here."

In response, they jabbed the pole at him, but it hit him right between the eyes. He fell back on the floor, rolled over, and held his bleeding nose. "You idiots. You jabbed me in the face."

"You said to jab it at you."

Unwisely, the other one said, "Boss, you look funny out there, and now, you're making red bubbles."

With the distraction, Izzy hurried past the beehive of activity around the soapy mess. At first, she tried to control her laughter, but it was too funny. Finally, she couldn't restrain it anymore. A burst of laughter escaped her.

The big boss hollered again from the middle the soapy mess. "Is someone laughing at me? You better not be laughing at me. You'll regret it."

He's getting what he deserves. Izzy wished that she could stay and watch, but eventually, they would get the situation under control.

That man deserves much worse. If only I could make things worse for him. The huckleberries would help. As she thought of the effects of huckleberries, an idea took root.

Izzy grinned so hard her cheeks hurt. Quickly, she ran to Annie's cage and said, "Annie, come here and swallow this."

She thrust her hand through one of the square holes of the cage and shoved the pill into the Annie's willing mouth. "Did you swallow it?"

"Yes, but it didn't taste very good."

Unfortunately, Izzy still had to swallow hers. Reluctantly, she looked at it. Izzy didn't like things that tasted bad.

The agent asked, "Did you both swallow the pills?"

Izzy forced herself to put the pill in her mouth, and, fighting against her gagging reaction, swallowed. She looked back at the agent and gave her a thumbs up gesture.

The agent ripped open the package and spun around throwing the berries into the soapy area. Immediately, everyone except Izzy and Annie let out a yell, "Berries!"

Everyone dove into the soapy area and began struggling to get and eat berries.

Annie said, "What are they doing?"

Izzy said, "Making a mess and after all of the berries have been eaten, they will run away from here." Her nose wrinkled at the disgusting thought of what would happen next.

"After they have run away, they'll all have terrible cases of diarrhea."

Annie said, "That sounds bad."

"Yes, bad for them. Wait here. I'll be right back."

Izzy ran from cage to cage freeing all the other animals. A terrible smell came from the berry fight. Purple bubbles had started coming from the struggle. The people and now the freed animals all fought for berries. The only sounds the people made were grunts.

One purple bubble drifted by Izzy. It smelled terrible. *That must be part of what the pill did.* She ran back to Annie's cage and freed her. Izzy shuddered at the thought of what came next. "Don't eat or lick anything purple."

"Why would I? The purple stuff smells terrible."

Izzy looked toward the ladder leading to the roof door. The soapy mess had spread all around the ladder. Relief at not having to climb the ladder warred with concern. *How am I going to get out of here?* Izzy remembered Annie could control gravity. She looked up at the roof door. *Annie could lift me up there.* Terrified, she looked around for another option.

The front door was out of the question. The soapy battle for berries had spread from the doorway. Animals were licking at the floor and some of the people were, too. Izzy remembered what had also fallen from the cages. *Ewww, that's terrible.*

Izzy had an inspiration. "Come on, Annie."

Together they ran to the back door. Before she opened it, she smelled the air. She could still smell the terrible odor of the huckleberries. She opened the door. Two guards turned to look at her. "They need help inside."

As the smell reached them, a crazed expression blossomed over their faces. The guards shoved past Izzy and Annie and ran inside.

Izzy sighed. "Well, that went good. Now, we just..." Izzy felt the blood leave her face. She remembered what the agent had said. Annie can take you to Noah.

~**********~

Annie raised one eyebrow and wrinkled her forehead. She looked at the young lady who had freed her. "What are we going to do?"

The lady didn't answer, and she looked uncomfortable and maybe afraid. In response, Annie leaned against her and licked her hand. The young woman looked down and said, "Thank you, Annie."

54

Annie asked, "You know my name. What's your name? What's wrong with you? You seem sad and frightened." Annie didn't really like to talk much, but humans didn't seem to get the other messages from tails, ears, eyes, and especially smells. As a result, Annie had decided humans needed more words. So Annie had learned to express herself with more words.

The young woman sighed. "My name is Izzy, and you're right. We need to go somewhere, and the idea is making me very frightened."

Annie thought the young woman's fear seemed to be getting worse. "Okay, let's go then. What are you frightened about?"

"We need to go a long way, and... "

After a long pause, Annie looked up at Izzy's troubled face. "You don't have to tell me about your fear if you don't want to. Where are we going?"

Izzy gave Annie a hug. She pulled a round device out of her pocket and pressed a button. A light lit up one edge. Izzy pointed south and said, "We need to go a long way in that direction. I was told you can help."

Annie gave Izzy a happy smile with her tongue hanging out. Annie decided that the woman's fear would get better once Annie started helping. Annie would show her how easy and quick it would be. It wouldn't take her long to get them up high and going south. Annie said, "Okay."

Annie had been helping her family go places for months until some bad people came and stole her. Annie thought the bad people needed more love in their lives. She tried to help the bad people, but she missed her family.

Her family had loved her. They loved Annie bringing home all kinds of things, like cars. Annie would even help them take things out of buildings and bring them home. She still wasn't sure about using gravity to rip the roof off the buildings called banks. Something about it bothered Annie.

Her tongue hung out in happy exuberance. Her tail wagged excitedly. Annie could hardly stand still. She loved helping. Annie had helped her family all the time.

Annie didn't like it when they went and got a car. It was hard for her to take cars through the sky. Her family always had her get cars at night.

Still, Annie liked helping people be happy. Using her ability to do the strange thing always made people happy. Annie felt the forces of gravity working on them and... Annie didn't know quite what she did, but... it was like a human turning off an electric light. Next, she used the things that gravity used to pull on them from above.

Annie didn't know she was breaking a law of physics and making it do what she wanted. She just did it. It made her happy to help. Now, the young lady she'd just met would be happy. It was easy to start them on the journey. It wouldn't take her long to lift her high into the air.

Izzy screamed. Her terror pulsed in each word. "The ground! What happened? Aaaah!"

Annie asked, "What's wrong? Did something happen to the ground? Are you okay?" It was hard for Annie to speak because of the death grip Izzy had on her. Annie liked being hugged, but this was ridiculous. It hurt. She'd done what the young woman wanted. Annie had them rapidly going hundreds of feet into the air and moving south at sixty miles per hour and going faster. *Why's Izzy frightened? Is something attacking us? What's wrong?* Annie tried to look around, but Izzy's death grip prevented her.

The answer from Izzy came quickly and with anger. "No, I'm not okay. This is terrifying."

"When my family had me take them places, the little ones had to shut their eyes until they got used to it."

As they talked, they lifted five hundred feet into the air and quickly picked up speed traveling south. The air felt fairly calm, but rising air or falling air bumped them every now and then. Below them, the city rushed past, until they passed over hills covered in pines. Next, they flew over fields. The yellow of ripe fields of grain carpeted the hills, interspersed with the brown of barren fields.

Izzy protested. "I am not going to get used to flying through the air."

"Okay. What do you want me to do? I could slow down or take us lower, but then I'll have to go slower and watch out for trees, wires, poles, wires, and birds. Well, not wires twice. I'll only have to watch for wires not wires and wires. Also, birds often don't like me flying by them. I apologize to them, but they still don't like it. Hawks and eagles are the worst. They try to attack me."

Izzy gasped, "I'm going to be sick. Take us down, quickly, please."

"Okay."

They plummeted back toward the ground. Annie picked a dirt road in the middle of a wheat field. Because of her hurry to please Izzy, they landed with more force than she normally did.

With Izzy's death grip on Annie, the dog had trouble with her landing, and they hit harder than she liked. Dust blew up around them, and they tumbled to a stop.

Izzy stopped crushing Annie in a death grip. Annie felt her move away and heard the young woman retching.

Annie got up and leaned against Izzy, nuzzling her head against her. "I'm sorry. Did I do something wrong? Is there something I can do? Your vomit smells good. Can I eat it?"

Between retching, Izzy responded by pushing Annie away. "No. Go away. Leave me alone. Ew, gross, don't eat my vomit. That's disgusting."

Annie backed away. The vomit smelled good to her. What was wrong with eating vomit? *I eat my own vomit.* This must be another strange human thing. *I have to be patient with her. That is part of loving.* Annie stretched out on the ground and laid her head on her front paws. Patiently, she watched and waited. The dust around them drifted away.

Eventually, Izzy stopped retching and looked at her. "Stop looking at me like that."

"Like what? I'm just waiting to find out what you want me to do next. I could lick your face."

"No, don't lick my face. Although I don't think it can get grosser than it is. Is there a house near here or a stream?"

Annie said, "There are houses scattered out in the fields. It would take us a long time to walk to any of them. There is also a stream farther away in the direction we are going. It would take us a very long time to walk to it. What do you want? I am getting thirsty. Are you getting thirsty?"

Izzy asked, "Why are you talking so much?"

Annie tipped her head to the side and looked at Izzy with a puzzled expression. The young woman's fear had dissipated, but she looked worn out and still a bit sick. She also sounded upset. "I've learned humans don't read my expressions very well and need me to talk with words to explain. We dogs communicate more without speaking. So, I have learned to speak more to help humans. I just want to make you happy. Don't you like me? I'm trying to be a good dog. I can talk less, but then you'll understand less. Humans seem to be slow that way."

At the last words, Izzy laughed. It was the best sound Annie had heard in a long time. She jumped up to her feet with her whole body wagging.

For other dogs, that action would show extreme pleasure.

58

Humans did seem to get a bit of that understanding. Annie bounded over to Izzy and stood up on her hind feet with her front paws on the young woman's shoulders. Annie started to lick her face but remembered just in time Izzy had refused that loving gesture. "I haven't heard human laughter in a long time. I love laughter unless I'm being laughed at. When humans laugh, they're happy. Although when I heard the very big boss laugh, it didn't sound good. Also, there was another person with very strange hair, and when she laughed, I felt sick. I think I'm going to like being with you. I miss my family. They would laugh when I got things for them like cars and things from banks. Although the first time I tried to get a car, I ripped it apart. They were upset and said I'd ruined the car. Could you be my new family?"

Izzy laughed long and loud. "You got cars for them? You really got something from a bank for them? Annie, I think I'm going to love you."

"Wonderful. I'm so excited. Are you sure you don't like having your face licked? Oh, also they had me get things from banks many times. I didn't like ripping the roofs off the banks. It seemed wrong."

"You ripped the roofs off banks? That is crazy. Yes, I'm sure I don't like having my face licked, and you're very heavy. Can you get your paws off my shoulders?"

"Okay." Annie jumped down and back. She looked intently at Izzy. "Do you want to start walking?"

Izzy sighed before she responded. "No, I need to get used to flying with you. Just don't lift me up until I say so. Okay?"

"Okay, are you ready? The river really looked good. We could go right now."

Izzy wiped the sweat off her forehead. "The river does sound good. First, let me get something out of my backpack. This heat is making me thirsty." Izzy shrugged out of her backpack and opened it, retrieving her water bottle. After a swig, she put it back. Izzy started to sling her backpack over her shoulder and stopped. "I'm sorry, Annie. I should've asked you if you're thirsty."

Annie said, "You are catching on to how I communicate without words. Yes, I'm thirsty, and I don't like this heat either. The bad people didn't give me enough water, but I can get us to the river quickly. Humans don't drink from the places I drink from. You should save your water, but thanks. You're nice. I'm happy to have you as my new family. Are you going to have me get cars?"

Izzy grinned. "No, I'm not going to have you get cars, and I'm not going to ask you to rip roofs off banks. That would be... crazy. I'm happy to have you, too, Annie. Do I need to be holding onto you when you move us with gravity?"

"No, I pick what objects for gravity to not pull on from below, then, I make gravity pull from above and from the direction I want us to go. In the past, I would pull lots of other things. It was very messy. In the very beginning, I didn't understand how to make gravity move things, and all I could do at first was to make things float. The first time, I terrified myself, but now I love it."

Izzy said, "Wow. That does sound kind of cool. Can you make us float, but keep us close to the ground?"

Annie said, "Yes, that's a good idea. The little kids loved playing with floating, and, after playing with floating, they did better at moving higher and faster."

Izzy said, "Okay, I'm ready." Her face showed surprise.

Annie carefully watched her expression. She remembered how terrified Izzy had been and how the little kids had easily gotten frightened.

Izzy pushed gently off the dirt road and drifted over the golden yellow of the wheat field.

Annie followed her. "Just tell me when you are going too high or too fast. I'll bring you back down or slow you down."

In a tremulous voice, Izzy responded, "Okay. This is amazing. If I don't move too fast, I can deal with this. New sports are easy for me. If I can control my fear, I can do this. I've got to. Others are counting on me. Unfortunately, I'm afraid of many things."

Annie asked, "You are? Why?"

Moving her arms, Izzy rotated to face Annie. "Please, don't repeat that to anyone else. I don't usually talk about my fears. My mom said it probably comes from when a robber broke into our home and shot my dad. She says I was there, but I don't remember what happened. A psychologist said my forgetting is a protective mechanism. It is called dissociative amnesia. It's very frustrating. I don't like being afraid."

"I'm sorry."

Izzy responded, "It isn't your fault. Can we stop talking about it?"

Annie circled around the slowly drifting Izzy. Only the gentle rustling of the wind blowing through the dry field of wheat broke the silence surrounding them. At first, Annie stayed at the same height as Izzy, but after going around Izzy twice, Annie started going higher and then lower.

Amazed, Izzy said, "How are you doing that? The gravity isn't affecting me, but just you."

"I control the gravity from below. For my body, I've added letting the gravity from above pull on just me very gently and then letting the gravity from below pull on just me very gently."

Izzy said, "That's incredible. You're amazing. What's the gravity from above? Are you creating gravity from above?"

Annie answered, "See the sun up above us? It is pulling on us. I didn't used to know that, but, now, I can feel it. Also, the moon is pulling from behind us. There are some others, but their gravity pull isn't as important, and I don't know what they are."

Izzy responded by flipping head over feet as she said, "This is amazing. You're amazing. Woops, I shouldn't have performed that flip."

Chapter Seven

The Chase

Weasels are 6 to 8.5 inches long plus their fairly short tail. They weigh 1.4 to 2 ounces. Gray squirrels are 9.1 to 11.8 inches long plus their almost equally long tail. They weigh 14 to 21 ounces. Squirrels should have nothing to fear. Wrong. Weasels have been known to kill prey 5 to 10 times their own size.

A squirrel's heartbeat goes from about 2 during hibernation to about 400 per minute during response to danger. It is no wonder squirrels cannot stay still when they are frightened.

The weasels split up. One gave orders. "Come at him from different directions. I'll wait for him down here."

P'Nut's heart revved back up, but this was too soon. He needed to rest more. *This isn't fair. I beat them. They should've left. The good guys are always supposed to win.* Instinct warned P'Nut of the deadliness of these foreign creatures. His muscles prepared for the new threat. P'Nut didn't worry about the men. They still had nets over their heads and struggled on the floor. P'Nut scolded, "Stay away. Stay away. Stay away."

The little squirrel could see the weasels' plan. *Are they weasels or woozles?* He continued to scold them. *I shouldn't be afraid of them. They're much smaller than me, but what can woozles do? Also, there are three of them.*

Plans and options to plans passed through his mind. One big obstacle was his condition. *I'm too tired for a long chase or battle. What would James Blonde do?* P'Nut's heart accelerated from two hundred and fifty to three hundred and fifty beats per minute. The men moved, trying to untangle from the nets and stand up.

The intent glares from the weasels' beady, little black eyes sent shivers of fear down P'Nut's back. His tail should've shaken more, but it couldn't. It had maxed out.

P'Nut remembered what his human friend had said. *He wanted me to escape, to use my strange vibrating way of moving through things. He wanted me to go outside.* The very thought of outside threatened his ability to reason. *Terrible things happen outside.*

The flanking weasels started climbing the bookshelf. They didn't move fast, just methodically.

P'Nut chose a plan. He ignored how tired he felt. *This has to work. I can still be fast.* He jumped for the chandelier. P'Nut reached out and clutched at an arm of it. This time, he heard more noise, worse noise from the ceiling. *Uh, oh, that noise isn't part of the plan. What does it mean?* The chandelier swung and spun. P'Nut had no time for fear or worry, only action.

Two weasels had reached his shelf. They watched with their beady little black eyes.

Something ripped free from above. P'Nut and the chandelier fell, spinning. His heart turbo-charged up to four hundred beats per minute. His muscles contracted, and he moved.

The weasel on the floor ran with one eye on P'Nut. *As soon as I land, it's going to jump me. The other two will be on me next.*

The chandelier continued to fall. P'Nut raced around on it.

P'Nut ducked under a loose wire and whipped his tail around to keep his balance. He jumped just before the chandelier crashed onto the slow-moving mass of men. Below him, the weasel reacted just fractions of a second slower than P'Nut.

It couldn't jump on P'Nut, not immediately at least. *I moved too slowly. That weasel could block my escape.* As P'Nut soared toward the ground, he saw the other weasels jumping down to close in on him. P'Nut brought his hind feet up to land. The vermin would have him boxed in. One limitation about vibrating came back to him. If another creature touched P'Nut before he vibrated it would join in his vibrating and travel with him.

Landing on all fours, P'Nut instantly pushed off and to the side. At the same time, he flicked his tail at the closest weasel jumping at him. It worked. The weasel slowed just a fraction, and P'Nut jumped over it.

P'Nut only had one thing going for him. He knew something they didn't. The weasels wouldn't expect him to jump at the wall. Who in their right mind jumped at walls?

The wall was straight ahead. A weasel advanced from the right. Another came from the left. P'Nut knew the third would've changed direction. They all would be right behind him.

As the little squirrel arced through the air, he said, in the deepest voice he could manage, "I'll be back."

Unfortunately, he really didn't know what the future held for him. It just seemed like the right thing to say before he left.

P'Nut landed just short of the wall. He continued straight at the wall running as fast as he could go. He had enough momentum to carry him through. *Outside, I've got to go outside. I'm going outside.* At the last terror-filled thought, he screamed, "Aaah!"

P'Nut vibrated, and the world turned blurry. P'Nut felt a strange feeling. His feet no longer ran on a surface. There was no surface. His feet churned. Desperately, P'Nut sought for something, anything, to grab. His legs churned freely as he flew through the wall.

The awe of seeing the inside of the wall stopped his screaming. *How do I do this?* P'Nut considered turning and running with the wall. He remembered his vibrating affected an area around him. *I've still got my jacket. If I was holding something, I could bring it with me. I can't get a grip on anything to change direction.*

P'Nut stopped trying to run. *Ha, ha, the weasels.* At that thought, the little squirrel remembered what had happened to the cat. P'Nut twisted his head back to watch.

The nearest weasel ran right at him. The strangeness of a squirrel vibrating and going right into a wall hadn't phased it in the least. Again, P'Nut wondered. *Are they weasels or woozles?*

P'Nut laughed at the sight of the woozle smashing headfirst into the wall. The other two piled into it from behind. All of them smashed their faces against the wall.

He laughed harder. P'Nut wished they could hear him laughing at them.

The moment of the humor and awe passed. P'Nut could no longer see them. The noises and sunlight of the outside hit the little squirrel. P'Nut stopped vibrating, laughing, and resumed screaming. He landed on grass. *Eww, grass.* The little squirrel hated grass almost as much as he feared the outside.

P'Nut saw his human friend sitting in a chair. Another man stood by his friend and held him down.

P'Nut wanted to race to his friend. His friend had always cared for him, but he hadn't been able to keep P'Nut safe from the bad people. P'Nut wanted to stay and fight the bad people. *James Blonde would fight them, but he had a gun and a license to kill. I don't want to kill anyone.*

More people stood farther away, watching. Out on the road, cars slowed down as they passed. The sunshine felt good. A gentle breeze blew through his fur. *This isn't so bad except for the grass.*

The little squirrel hopped across the horrible grass. Each time P'Nut landed and felt the grass, he immediately leapt out of it. With the last leap, P'Nut jumped out of the nasty grass and onto a plastic, pink flamingo stuck in the grass. It swung slightly back and forth. From the new vantage point, P'Nut studied the situation. He didn't see the dog. That was good. *It's not so bad out here. It's actually nice. The sun is nice. I like that breeze. I could rest. If only I hadn't failed my mission of getting the bad people to leave.* P'Nut decided to scold the bad man. Scolding was always a good choice.

A barking voice ruined his moment. "I'm coming, Master. I'm coming."

At that moment, two things happened. First, the terrible dog charged around the corner of the house. Grass flew from under his paws as the massive dog raced. He trailed a taut leash.

Secondly, the door of his old home opened. P'Nut heard the little woman scream. "Get him."

The dog jumped over a big stump. *He's running slower than normal. He's sprinting, but he's not gaining much speed.*

The end of the long, taut leash came around the corner of the house. That revealed why the terrible dog ran so slowly.

A small man, lying on the ground, held the leash. He slid around the corner of the house on his belly. The man swung across the grass. He rolled multiple times. Finally, the man rolled back onto his belly, face down.

The man looked up. He spit out some grass. All the time, he stubbornly held onto the leash.

The three weasels dashed out of the house, and immediately, they charged at the little squirrel perched on the pink flamingo.

The dog yelled, "Master, I'm coming. Let go of my master. I'll bite you." He swerved toward where his master fought to get out of the chair.

The leash angled away from the stump. The man slid on the grass into a new course.

The dog must've seen P'Nut at that moment, because he changed direction. "Squirrel, squirrel, I'll catch it." He sprinted faster, throwing more clumps of grass behind him. The leash angled back over the stump.

The little squirrel's nightmare had returned. P'Nut had no time to decide what to do.

The sliding man's eyes went wide. He said, "Oh, no." He slid right at the stump.

P'Nut saw a terrified expression on the man's face. *Poor man, he must've seen the stump.*

Before the man could let go of the leash, he slammed into the stump with a horrible thump. The leash whipped free. Loose from the burden, the terrible dog picked up speed. Two other men ran around the house after him.

Plans and options to plans for escaping rattled around in the terrified little squirrel's mind. P'Nut couldn't think of a viable option. First, he really didn't want to jump back down onto the grass. *Eww, grass.*

The weasels covered half the distance to P'Nut.

Second, the dog really frightened P'Nut. That dog ran too fast. The dog would reach him first. Maybe, he could jump and land on its back. The terror kept P'Nut from making a quick choice.

Then, his friend yelled at the dog. "Fido, get those vermin chasing P'Nut."

Before his friend finished speaking, P'Nut jumped off the pink flamingo. He raced for the road. "Bye, friend, and thanks for all the nuts."

Fido always obeys except when he gets really excited. He really gets excited by chasing squirrels and that means me. If only, there was a tree. P'Nut would be safe in a tree. Desperately, he looked for something, anything, to use in case the terrible dog didn't obey.

Fido yelled. Fido always yelled. "Yes, Master-human-god. I'll get those vermin. Bye, P'Nut. No hard feelings about your tail?"

"None, well, not many. Thanks for chasing the vermin." At another thought, P'Nut added, "Don't bite these bad people. They'll use it as an excuse to kill you." P'Nut ran as he talked, but he'd also watched the weasels. They were gaining. *I'm slowing down. They'll catch me.*

A person on a bicycle pedaled toward the people watching on the sidewalk. The biker yelled, "Get off the sidewalk. What are you watching?"

P'Nut changed his direction. *I won't make it to the road, but...* He jumped and landed on the bicycle rider.

The biker yelled, "Eww a rat. Get off me, rat."

The little squirrel ran up the person's back. "I'm a squirrel, not a rat." He added, "Sorry. Sorry." The weasels were falling behind. He scolded them, "Give up. You're never going to get me."

The weasel in the lead answered, "I promise we will get you."

P'Nut ignored her threat and relaxed, enjoying a welcome break from running. He turned his face into the wind and enjoyed how it puffed his cheek pockets out. Unfortunately, the person peddling the bike acted weird.

The bike wobbled. "Get off me, rat."

"I'm not a rat. I'm not a rat."

Ahead of them, P'Nut saw a person painting a fire hydrant red. A dog walked up, checking out the fire hydrant. The painter waved his paint brush at it.

P'Nut tried to warn everyone. "Look out."

The biker asked, "What?"

The dog looked up and jumped back.

P'Nut felt the bike slow. It wasn't enough. *At least the dog is smart. Hopefully, the others won't get hurt.*

The squirrel jumped. P'Nut heard the crash and a splash. He looked back. Red paint dripped off the biker and the painter. The dog just walked up and sniffed at the fire hydrant.

P'Nut also saw the weasels. They had spread out. The weasels still raced after him.

The little squirrel raced onto the road. P'Nut had gained a valuable lead on the weasels. He heard screeching brakes.

Time for P'Nut froze. The little squirrel remembered long ago other screeching brakes and his mother getting killed.

The car swerved toward him. *They're trying to kill me.* The shock of their cruelty and the hot breath of the nearest weasel got P'Nut moving again. He raced under the vehicle. He would've crouched there in terror at the size and noise of the car, but one weasel had followed him. *It stinks under here and not just from that evil creature.*

One of the wheels hit a pothole and water splashed up. P'Nut saw the muddy water splash toward him. *Not my jacket.* The little squirrel shifted directions and darted out between the tires on the other side.

P'Nut sighed in relief when he realized his jacket was safe. He jumped over another pothole. Other cars honked their horns. More blaring of horns and screeching of brakes filled the air. A drenched weasel ran out from under the car. *Ha. He wasn't as fast as me.*

The squirrel heard a crashing sound. P'Nut wanted to scold the cars for honking at him and trying to run him over, but he didn't think it would do any good. Instead, as the cars roared up, P'Nut focused on running as if his life depended on his speed and avoiding the cars. *My life does depend on me moving fast. If these cars don't get me, I expect one of these nasty weasels or woozles will get me. I've got to get out of here and find somewhere to eat and rest.*

After the crashing sound, P'Nut heard people yelling. The little squirrel ignored them. All he could see was cars and weasels chasing him. *I need to get up higher.*

P'Nut ran off the road and onto a narrow strip of dirt and plants between the first road and a second road. He'd been in a car before. P'Nut had a general idea of what it was like. One of his eyes caught sight of a weasel closing in on him. The cars no longer raced as fast.

Another crashing sound blasted through the other noise. *These cars are not safe. They should stop moving.*

On the new road, a small car moved around another car. The small car would pass right in front of him. P'Nut jumped. He landed on the hood and slid toward the windshield. The little squirrel caught sight of two startled faces. P'Nut jumped and vibrated through the windshield.

The man yelled, "Ah, get out of here."

The woman asked, "Did you see what that squirrel just did?"

What's the crazy human talking about? Of course, he saw me. He's sitting right there. During the yells and thoughts flashing through P'Nut's head, he landed on the back seat. He felt the car slowing. *That's too bad. I hoped they would get me out of here.*

Quickly, P'Nut jumped and jumped again to the dashboard. He

turned around and said, "Thanks for the lift."

In a slightly less terrified voice, the man said, "I can't get used to understanding animals."

Two more cars crashed into each other. P'Nut glimpsed Fido chasing a weasel between the cars on the new road. The little squirrel mentally thanked the brown dog. *If I survive, I'll have to thank Fido. I couldn't have made it this far without his help.*

A weasel jumped onto the hood of the car and slid up to the window. The driver turned on the windshield wipers. The weasel grabbed one and swiped back and forth. All the time, it stared at P'Nut.

The man screamed, "This is freaking me out!"

The woman said, "You look very cute in your suit jacket."

P'Nut brushed a paw over his jacket. He loved his jacket. "Thanks. Thanks. You're attractive, too. Do you have any nuts? Also, some water would be great if you have it."

Rest and some food would be a help, but he knew this car could only give him temporary safety. If she had a jar of nuts, maybe she'd know how the nuts got into the jar. No one had ever answered that question.

The car continued to slow to a stop, and now the driver door started opening. *That's bad, very bad.*

P'Nut saw a telephone pole on the other side of the road. He had watched other squirrels climbing telephone poles and running along the wires. P'Nut had an idea. He said to the woman, "You deserve someone better than him." He added, "Bye. Bye" as he raced across the dashboard in front of her and vibrated through her door.

Somehow, the third weasel waited on that side of the car. Terror pulsed through P'Nut. Fortunately, he reacted faster than the weasel, but the chase was on again. *Do woozles or weasels ever get tired?*

P'Nut darted under the stopped car next to them. He dashed out the other side. *I've got to get to that telephone pole.* This plan all rested on how well the woozles could climb, but first, he had to get to the pole. P'Nut came out the other side at full speed. *I've got to take a break.*

He knew he couldn't keep this up for much longer. What he saw made his hope vanish.

Another weasel ran at him from that side. It blocked his way to the pole. P'Nut leapt. That weasel jumped. P'Nut flicked his tail to avoid its leap. A different weasel spotted the goal of P'Nut's jump and raced to get there first.

P'Nut checked the distance against his speed, forward momentum, and how high he had managed to jump. *I won't reach the pole.*

The little squirrel bared his teeth. Below, the weasel bared its teeth. *This is a disaster. All three against me at the same time. What can I do?*

"Someone, anyone, help me. Help me."

P'Nut landed on a big, brown, furry back. Instantly, he started to scratch and bite. Nothing bit back. He heard a voice, a loud yelling voice. *Who always yells?*

In his terror, P'Nut hadn't realized he had landed two feet above the ground. A weasel to the left leapt at him. Another to the right leapt. P'Nut jumped for the pole.

The voice continued yelling. "I'll get you, vermin. Go, P'Nut. Escape. Tell Master-god that I was a good doggy."

P'Nut landed. He raced up the pole, whipped around it, and looked down.

What P'Nut saw froze the marrow in his bones. Fido struggled against the three weasels. He couldn't seem to bite any of them. In turn, they mostly didn't seem to be hurting Fido. One rode on the big brown dog's back. The size difference was almost humorous.

For the first time in his life, P'Nut found himself speechless.

That weasel or woozle gnawed at the base of Fido's head. *Woozles are bad.* Without realizing it or thinking about it, P'Nut had started back down the pole. He froze in terror. *They aren't really hurting Fido.* An image of the three of them swarming himself drove him back. *No! Fido was helping me.*

P'Nut descended. "Let him alone. Let him alone. I'm the one you're supposed to get. Are you so dumb that you can't remember? Let him—" The little squirrel broke off in mid scolding.

The fight changed even as the little squirrel scolded. Fido flipped and rolled. All the while, he snapped his teeth at the three vicious, little animals.

As if they had synchronized their timing, the three vermin broke free from Fido and jumped for the pole.

P'Nut whipped around from his upside-down position and raced up the pole. From below, he heard Fido.

"Go, P'Nut. You're faster. If they try to come back down, I'll chomp them to pieces."

Fido continued yelling, but P'Nut stopped listening. Whenever the dog started yelling, he never seemed to know when to stop.

P'Nut raced to the top of the pole and jumped onto a wire. He ran for a little way and looked back. The little squirrel whipped its tail back and forth to maintain his balance. Behind him, the first weasel followed. It came much slower than P'Nut could move, but with its beady black eyes fixed on the little squirrel, it continued the hunt.

P'Nut said, "Why don't you give up?"

The lead weasel said, "Because we're going to get you. We never fail."

Instantly, P'Nut whirled around and resumed running. *Those creatures are crazy.* The wire led to a building, but there was a tree, a lovely tree. The little squirrel knew that the tree had food. It was the same as another one he'd seen squirrels in.

Branches of the tree were below P'Nut and only eight feet away. He ran forward and leapt out to the side. He leapt with his front legs out and his hind legs and tail stretched out behind him. Without thinking, P'Nut waved his tail to keep on target. At the end of the jump, he brought his tail up. That rotated his body up, and he brought his hind feet forward. Leaves and twigs ripped past. Too late, P'Nut thought of his jacket. *My jacket, its buttons, it might snag on something or get damaged.* He landed on his target and crouched to relieve some of the impact.

Immediately, P'Nut sat up. With his paws, he checked his jacket for any damage. He sighed in relief and spun to check on his pursuers. The three weasels stared back from the wire. The jump wasn't one they dared to take. "Ha, ha, ha, ha, ha, ha you can't get me. You look foolish all lined up with nowhere to go. Ha, ha, ha, ha, ha." P'Nut turned and flicked his tail at them. "Now, you'll have to give up."

The lead weasel stared at him and answered, "Never."

P'Nut shuddered at the crazy animal's refusal. He gave a big sigh. *They can't get me.* It felt so good to leave the chaos behind. Finally, he would get some food and rest. Afterwards, he would figure out what to do next. Maybe the bad guys would give up and leave. He didn't believe the crazy woozles would give up.

An angry scolding tore him from the pleasure of nibbling on a bud.

"This is my tree. This is my tree. Get out of my tree. Get out of my tree." The owner of the voice jumped, leapt, and ran through the branches of the tree.

The other squirrel seemed bigger, and P'Nut knew he had only one option. The little squirrel raced through the tree with the other close behind. *Not another chase.* P'Nut knew he moved too slowly to get away, but the other squirrel seemed content just to chase him. Also, P'Nut found it very easy to race through the tree. The vibrissae on his legs told him about the tree limbs and branches he raced over. It would've been fun if he wasn't so tired. P'Nut took advantage of the situation to slow down more. *I need to rest.*

Unfortunately, the pace of the chase also gave him more opportunity to think. He hated having to run away. *What else could I have done? My friend wanted me to escape. I failed my mission. I like to pretend to be like those heroes in movies, but the truth is I'm not. I'm just a little rodent.*

Chapter Eight

The Secret Agent

Eastern Gray Squirrels have excellent memories. They will remember solutions to problems and the locations of thousands of nuts. Also, they can't see the color red. Remember, for squirrels, red looks like yellowish-green. That means squirrels don't see purple the way we do.

P'Nut leapt from the tree to the roof of a building. More scolding came from behind him. "Don't come back. This is my tree. Don't come back."

The little squirrel turned and responded. "Yeah, yeah, it's your tree. It's your tree. Don't get your tail in a knot."

At the same time, P'Nut looked for the woozles or weasels. *Which is it? Are they weasels or woozles?* He couldn't see them or Fido. P'Nut tried to remember if he had heard Fido yelling, but he couldn't remember hearing anything. From his vantage point, everything seemed peaceful. *Finally, I've left the chaos behind.*

P'Nut paused for a moment to smooth his jacket. Carefully, he brushed it. Satisfied, he twitched his tail and slowly scampered across the long roof. The little squirrel didn't recognize anything around him. *How far have I gone? I'm a long way from home.* Many new odors drifted to him. One of them tried to get his attention, but a voice startled and distracted him. P'Nut jumped.

"Hello there. You look lost. Are you new to this area?"

A starling perched on the edge of a roof about twenty feet away. It asked, "Well?"

At first, P'Nut didn't know what to say. Finally, he answered, "Who are you? Who are you?"

"You squirrels always repeat yourselves. Why do you do that? You look hungry and tired."

"I don't always repeat myself. I..." *I might.* "Do you know where some food is?" Again, something tried to get his attention. A wonderful memory tickled at the back of his mind. *What is it?*

"You look hungry." The starling stopped to preen some feathers before he continued. "I might know of some possibilities. Most of them already have squirrels that would chase you away. I don't recognize you. You're new to this area, aren't you? Where are you from? I could try to help..."

P'Nut was tired, thirsty, and hungry. He hoped this bird would help. "I—"

Two more starlings joined the first. They interrupted P'Nut. "Is this the one?"

"I don't know. I was just trying to find out. Now, you have probably fouled up my efforts."

"Look. He has a short tail just like our boss said."

"I think it's him. This is great. We found him quickly."

P'Nut looked back and forth at the birds. "What are you talking about?"

"Yeah, I think you're right. I haven't seen another squirrel missing the end of its tail. Black, you go back and tell the client we've spotted their quarry. Make sure they pay our flock the food, and then lead them back here."

The other one said, "They might send those nasty weasels. I don't trust them. They'd eat any of us if they could."

P'Nut listened carefully, hoping the conversation would tell him where food was, but the more he listened, the more he worried about what they said. When he heard about weasels, he froze.

The shock dissipated. P'Nut took off. He finished his run to the end of the roof. As he reached the end of the roof, a smell that had been trying to get his attention succeeded. *I know that smell.* Food, delicious, wonderful food beckoned to him. He lifted his nose into the gentle breeze and inhaled deeply. *Is that french fries?* Behind him came the calls of the starlings.

"He's leaving."

"Follow him. I'll wait here."

"I'll be back as soon as we get paid. Don't lose sight of him."

"Lose sight of him? We're birds. How could he hide from us? He's just a squirrel. They aren't as sneaky as rats."

Those smells and the memory overrode his consideration of the bird calls. His stomach wanted whatever made that tantalizing smell. *I smell french fries.* He had never gotten enough french fries. Across the next street, P'Nut saw a building with cars around it. People walked up to a door, opened it, and entered the building. Through the windows, P'Nut saw people sitting at tables. On the tables, he saw a wondrous sight. Food. They had food and a lot of it.

The birds wouldn't follow him into a building. *I could hide in there. More importantly, I could eat french fries if they have them, but it did smell like french fries.* Many times, his friends had fed him at their table while they ate. They enjoyed P'Nut eating with them. This would be fun. P'Nut could imagine himself at one of the tables, tasting the food and chatting. He liked chatting with people.

P'Nut took off for the building. He didn't worry about the bird following him. It wouldn't be able to follow him into the building. He'd fool it.

Happily, he continued to consider how much he would enjoy eating, drinking, and chatting. One tall man, something about him seemed strange to P'Nut, stopped and looked up at him. The man wore a nice suit jacket similar to his own. *Why's he looking at me?* The tall man turned and entered the building.

Jumping and leaping, P'Nut raced from the roof and onto a wire leading to one of the tall poles. With another jump, he leapt to a different wire and raced over the road below. The little squirrel couldn't wait to get into this building. *What other food will they have? What will it be like in there? Will they really have french fries? I love french fries. What about grapes? At the thought of juicy, tender, plump grapes, P'Nut stopped running and looked into the nearer windows.* He imagined how one of the young ladies would feed him grapes. Normally, a few, certain nuts would've been high on his list, but thirst pushed grapes past them.

They would smile and tell me how cute I am. I would reach my paws out and take their treasured offering. I would tell them "thank you." Then, I would sink my teeth into the juicy... P'Nut stopped thinking. He couldn't think of words awesome enough to express how he felt about grapes.

Briefly, the thought of how the biker had reacted made him think of different possibilities about how these people might react. Also, the thought of how the people in the car had reacted flashed through his mind. For some reason, the tall, unusual man came to his thoughts. The little squirrel ignored the warnings of his own memories.

P'Nut jumped onto a nearby pole. He turned his paws backwards and raced head first down the pole. He jumped the last six feet and raced around the corner of the building.

The food was so close. P'Nut had thought to be more careful

about entering the restaurant, but the closer he got, the more he just wanted to hurry. *I've looked through the windows. I know where the floor is and...* P'Nut stopped thinking.

Quickly, before the bird could see what he did, P'Nut jumped and vibrated through the wall. Conversation, noises, talking, and most of all, the wonderful fragrances of food hit him. To his left, he saw a small french fry on the floor. Not as awesome as grapes, but it would definitely do for starters. P'Nut sighed. *Oh, glorious and wonderful food.* His friend had limited P'Nut to only one small french fry at a time as a special treat. He'd told P'Nut that french fries were bad for squirrels. *How can something that smells so good be bad?*

P'Nut grabbed the french fry up in his paws, sat down, and ate the delicious food. The wonderful morsel finished, P'Nut sighed and looked around for more food.

Nothing. There wasn't any more food on the floor. The only problem about the french fry was that it had made him thirstier. P'Nut carefully cleaned his paws, started smoothing his fur and his jacket. *It is time for me to go up and enjoy some time with these people.*

P'Nut felt a familiar uncomfortable feeling and then a toot from the base of his tail. Uh *oh, my friends didn't like me tooting while they ate, although kids laugh at it.* P'Nut hadn't seen any kids around the tables. The little squirrel didn't feel so confident about jumping up and talking to complete strangers. *What do I know about people? My friend, his family, and their friends treated me nicely.* P'Nut thought of all the new people he'd met this day. This time, he considered their reactions. *None of them had liked me or treated me nice. None of them, except that one lady, had—*

A small round object dropped to the floor. The object interrupted his thoughts. P'Nut stared. The grape bounced.

P'Nut's eyes widened with joy and anticipation. His heart rate picked up. He rose to lunge for it.

The grape descended. His paws reached as he started to move. In horror, P'Nut saw something else. He desperately wanted to save the round treasure.

A shoe descended. P'Nut stopped just in time. The shoe smashed the grape. Juice, precious juice, squirted out. The grape was gone. P'Nut considered going over and licking up the juice, but it wouldn't be the same as holding the perfect treasure in his paws. Another french fry fell to the floor, but P'Nut ignored it. *There are more grapes up there.* He remembered his friend telling him how suave P'Nut could be.

P'Nut remembered asking what "suave" meant. They'd watched a movie together. His friend had said the actor was suave. P'Nut remembered that actor saying his name was Blonde, James Blonde.

The little squirrel remembered how he'd copied the actor. *The name is P, P'Nut.* Of course, his squeaky voice wasn't quite the same as the actor's, but his friend had loved it. *I am suave. I can be...*

P'Nut looked up at the table where the treasure had fallen from. Before he could have any more discouraging or careful thoughts, P'Nut leapt from the floor to the table.

Before he could introduce himself with his prepared introduction of "Hello, I'm P, P'Nut," the two ladies sitting at the table jumped to their feet and screamed.

"Ahhh, there's a rat."

P'Nut didn't expect the scream. He wanted to object to being referred to as a rat. Instead, P'Nut decided to go full James Blonde.

The little squirrel reached out a paw to a fancy stemware glass filled with liquid. As low as he could get his squeaky voice to go, P'Nut said, "The name's Blonde, James Blonde."

Meanwhile, the uproar in the room grew louder.

"I demand to talk to your manager."

"Someone, get rid of that rodent."

Other voices were less strident.

"Look at that little actor."

"Where did it learn that?"

"Take a picture of him."

"Look at his jacket."

"How cute."

"He isn't a rat. He's a cute squirrel."

But the more strident and complaining voices seemed to be winning.

"Someone needs to get rid of that rodent."

"This is disgusting."

"I'm going to complain."

"I demand that you remove this... this rodent."

P'Nut looked at the plate of food next to him. He didn't know what much of it was, but it smelled good. The things he did recognize and yearned for were the grapes. One, on the edge of the plate, was just inches from him. It would be so easy to grab it and eat it. The temptation was so great, but P'Nut had been taught that it wasn't polite to take food off someone else's plate. He also didn't think it would be suave to steal the food from the plate.

Four people advanced on him. "Okay, little troublemaker, you need to come with us."

P'Nut didn't know what he could do. His hope was almost gone.

Weakly, he tried again. "I'm not a troublemaker. I'm... I'm... The name is Blonde, James Blonde."

From a table back in a corner of the restaurant, a deep, clear, and surprisingly calm voice cut through the commotion and uproar. The voice sounded confident and full of authority.

"If everyone will calm down, I will pay for all of your meals. James Blonde, I would like you to join me at my table. Everyone else, sit down."

The last words had the ring of a command. The strident, yelling voices stopped. Everyone sat down. One lady missed her chair and sat on the floor.

P'Nut didn't know what to do. One of the four people, who had been advancing on him held a round, silver tray. She held it out to him, and said, "Mr. Blonde, if you would like, jump on this tray, and I will carry you to the gentleman's table."

P'Nut looked at the grapes on the plate by him. He looked at the ladies. Now, they sat at the table with red faces. He bowed and said, "Ladies, please excuse me for bothering you. Enjoy your food."

With that, the little squirrel jumped lightly onto the tray. It wobbled a little, but the young lady managed it. She turned and carried him in front of her toward the gentleman's table in the far corner. What happened next surprised P'Nut and warmed his heart.

Someone started clapping. Others joined in. P'Nut heard one of the ladies from the table he'd jumped on. "Sorry, Mr. Blonde, for screaming."

The little squirrel stood up straight on his hind feet and bowed to the left and to the right. The applause increased before dying off.

P'Nut looked at the man they carried him to. The man, with neat dark hair and wearing a fancy suit, gazed back, unblinking. The stare unnerved the little squirrel. It was the tall and unusual man who'd looked at him outside. *What does this man want with me? How come he isn't blinking?*

Gently, the lady set the silver tray on the corner table. "Here he is, sir."

The tall man at the table said, "Thank you." He turned to look at P'Nut and said, "You may call me 'Bond.'" Bond asked, "Would you like something to eat?"

"Some grapes and maybe some nuts if that isn't too much to ask for please. Oh, and some water, shaken not stirred."

The waitress asked in a confused voice, "What? Shaken water?"

Mr. Bond said, "I think he is making a reference to the movie character James Blonde."

The waitress listened to what the tall man said, and the confusion on her face cleared. "Oh, of course." She laughed and said, "I'll be right back with your water, and I'll shake it and not stir it." She laughed again.

Some in the room still looked at P'Nut, but most of the room had returned to a normal hum of eating and talking.

P'Nut turned to the man and asked, "Do you expect me to talk?"

"No, I expect you to live. You see, little Blonde, I have need of your help."

Of everything that had happened during the day, this surprised P'Nut the most. He squeaked, "You... need my help? You need my help?" Recovering quickly, he added, "Yes. What do you need?" The little squirrel started to repeat himself, but the surprisingly quick delivery of food interrupted his talking. The nuts looked just like the ones from a jar. *Maybe this waitress knows how nuts get into a jar.*

As he ate, the man filled him in. "Do you prefer Blonde or P'Nut."

P'Nut didn't want to take the grape from his mouth to answer, so he just shrugged. *Wait. How did he know my name?*

Bond lowered his voice, "You see, P'Nut, I have a problem, but I also have many, many sensors feeding my computer programs. You see, little squirrel, unlike you, I am not really alive. I am a part of an artificial intelligence, an AI, which has a problem. I am a robot, an appendage of this AI."

At this announcement, P'Nut just sagely nodded his head. *What's he talking about?*

"I do not know how much of this you will understand, but this is what it boils down to. There are many trying to take advantage of the turmoil caused by the arrival of aliens, the aliens telling us of the need to train heroes to save us from a new enemy, the new ability of every living thing to understand every other living thing, and the amazing things some living creatures like you can now do by playing with physics. It has come to my attention that in the near term, one organization trying to gain power during this time of chaos is after a very special crystal. Unfortunately, I do not have the ability to safeguard that crystal on my own. A video on the internet of your miraculous escape caught my attention. Did you know that there are hundreds of videos about you on the internet? You are quite the star."

P'Nut didn't know what to say. He chose to just nod and eat.

The man continued. "More importantly, I recognized you have an innate ability to examine a situation and build a plan to defeat your enemies. Examining those videos made me realize that with your abilities, you can save us in this dangerous situation. You can be the hero that everyone needs."

At the last words, P'Nut gagged on the grape pulp he'd just started to swallow. His gagging must've worried the man, because the man stopped speaking and looked at him in concern.

Chapter Nine

Chaos and Escape

Artificial Intelligence (AI) is quickly advancing, but it is still limited at this point, and hopefully, it always will be. At this point, advanced AI is limited to huge processing locations and uses massive amounts of power. Quantum computing could change this.

P'Nut swallowed and said, "Me, a hero? I'm not a hero. I've been terrified for most of the day. I failed to get the bad people to leave my home. I had to escape. I had to escape. I just pretended to be like James Blonde. Haven't you noticed how small I am? Why don't you have another human do this? They can do much more than I can."

"Little squirrel, being a hero is not about *not* being terrified. It is not about size. Being a hero is about being terrified and still doing what needs to be done. I watched you today. You were amazing, and the chaos you can create will be perfect for my plan. Also, those bad people left your home after you escaped."

Neither spoke. P'Nut nibbled on a nut. He really wasn't hungry anymore. The news about the bad people leaving made him feel much better. *What's the other stuff he's talking about? Artificial intelligence? Computers?* P'Nut realized Bond hadn't answered his question about using a human. Just then the man answered.

"There is a human that is working with me, but she is too far away. She thinks I should get the crystal to a young man named Noah. She is also working to get a very special dog to him. This is a picture of Noah."

Bond placed a flat sheet on the table. It had some words and a picture on it. The man tapped on the sheet and the picture of a tall, thin young man with yellowish-green hair appeared. "Trying to get the crystal to this Noah is a very dangerous idea. I have decided on a much safer plan, and you will fit into this plan perfectly. I will be watching and will try to provide help when I can. Now, this is what I need you to do. In a little bit, there is going to be a big commotion. Use it to escape back into the kitchen."

Bond tapped the sheet. A new picture appeared of a truck. "This delivery truck is out back. When we are done here, you will go through the kitchen to the back door and go to this truck. In the back of it are boxes. Get into one of the boxes of vegetables. The truck will take you to an airport and will deliver the rest of the vegetables to an airline caterer."

Each time he talked of something new, Bond tapped on the sheet, and a new picture appeared.

P'Nut had a thought. "Sorry to interrupt, but what am I going to do to protect this crystal? Isn't there anyone else that can do this?"

"That is a smart fellow. All you have to do is to create a big disturbance on the plane. This will cause the plane to return to the airport. In the meantime, I will finish getting a small, trustworthy part of the government the authority they need to recover the crystal from the plane."

Bond reached across to P'Nut with something small. "This small device will allow me track you. I am pinning it to your jacket. I will get help to you when I can."

Bond reached across with some other small objects. "These are cufflinks for your suit jacket. Tap on them three times in quick succession, and little flying things will attack those nearest you." He snapped them onto the fake white sleeves sewn inside of P'Nut's suit.

Tap on them three times, got it. They look nice on my shirt

88

sleeves. Bond didn't answer my question.

The man reached across with a small pea-sized object and carefully put it into a small pocket in P'Nut's suit. "This is something you might find useful to create chaos. It is a small huckleberry with a special coating. To use it, get it wet and throw it or drop it and run away from it. All people and animals near it will go crazy." He put a small pill in a pocket on the other side of P'Nut's suit. "Be sure to eat some of this pill before you get the huckleberry wet, or you will go crazy. That would be bad, and whatever you do, do not eat any part of the berry or its juice."

Eat some of pill and get berry wet and throw it away. I love berries. It seems like a waste to throw it away.

P'Nut decided to ask again. "Isn't there any other human who can keep the crystal safe?"

Bond looked at him in silence before replying. "I did have a very trustworthy helper. She was my friend, at least, how I understand the concept of a friend. She died. The people trying to get the crystal killed her. Please, you have to help. Do not let her life be given in vain. This should not be very dangerous for you."

The little squirrel searched his memory for a James Blonde reply to this serious request. He couldn't remember one that would work. Instead, he said, "I've only got one life to live. Using that life to be a hero sounds good to me. I would rather just not end up as a dead hero."

"And I would rather you do not end up dead. When I can, I will help. Now, we're running out of time. Let us go over the rest."

The man talked faster. After talking about the caterer and what to expect, Bond tapped on the sheet again. A picture appeared of an airline trolley.

Bond said, "This is important. You need to get into this trolley. Memorize what this one looks like. See that—" The man had pointed down at the corner of the trolley.

P'Nut interrupted. "That mark down at the bottom looks unique from the others you showed me."

"Yes, exactly. The bottom of the trolley will have room for you. You have to stay quiet until after you are lifted into the plane. It will be loaded onto a jet. I will contact you when you should start creating chaos." At each step, Bond had tapped the sheet on the table. It displayed different pictures and finally a container. "This container will be below you in a cargo hold."

Bond tapped the sheet again and a picture appeared of a crystal on a necklace. "This purple crystal will be in that container. Your chaos will cause the plane to return to the airport, and we will then be able to retrieve you and the crystal."

What's a plane? What's a jet? Does the plane get loaded into the jet? P'Nut tried to look like he understood but questions built.

P'Nut had looked attentively at each picture. He looked carefully at the off-shade blue crystal. *Me? A hero?* Finally, some questions had to be asked. "How will I know who a bad guy is? Why do you trust me?"

"They do not like animals or other people really. They will try to get the crystal. They only want power. I trust you because having you help is giving the highest probability of success, and I think you are a good guy. In fact, I think you are just the hero I need. Probabilities are how I make my decisions. Speaking of which, you might run into one of the bad people on the plane. They will probably have at least one person on the flight. Stay in the trolley until I contact you. Then start causing chaos."

They don't like animals? What's a plane? Maybe it's another word for jet. The comment about the bad guys not liking animals made P'Nut think of the people back at his home and the woozles or weasels. "Do you know what woozles are?"

At his question, confusion crossed the face of the man or whatever he was. "Uh... Maybe you are referring to the fictional woozles of the Winnie the Pooh story?"

P'Nut understood the look of confusion. He sympathized. "Winnie the Pooh? Who's that?" *Woozles are just fictional-not real, but these weasels are real.* Vaguely, P'Nut remembered seeing a movie about Pooh. *I got things mixed up. I better ask about those things I don't understand.* "Bond, what—"

At that moment, the door opened, and chaos in the form of the starlings and weasels flowed into the restaurant. One of the starlings said, "There he is."

The three weasels ran toward P'Nut. A man near the door yelled, "Hey. You animals aren't allowed in here."

The starlings flew to tables and started helping themselves to food. People started screaming. For some reason, the birds didn't like people shooing them away.

Bond pointed and said, "Go to the kitchen. Remember what I told you. Do not let the purple crystal get into the hands of the bad people. I will delay these scoundrels."

P'Nut turned to jump, but before he did, Bond moved very fast. He picked up the silver tray and flung it at a weasel. The weasel ducked under a chair. The tray missed, skipped off the floor, arched up and shattered a water pitcher one of the waiters carried. The water drenched one of the starlings that had attacked a young lady and stolen a beak full of her food.

The tray dropped back down aimed right at another weasel. The blood thirsty creature jumped out of the way just in time.

Bond's voice cut like a knife through the chaos. "Everyone, help Blonde. He is a special agent. These creatures after him are evil."

As P'Nut jumped, he saw someone throw their plate of food at a weasel. Unfortunately, it missed and hit a server carrying a big platter with dishes of food. The unfortunate server stumbled and almost lost control of the platter.

P'Nut watched the room dissolve into chaos as he searched out a path. Other people threw dishes, glasses, and silverware at the weasels and starlings. Unfortunately, they did not have good aims. P'Nut ran and jumped onto a table. Just in time, he ducked to avoid a dish flying past him. "Sorry, excuse me."

The wet starling flapped up into the air. A young lady picked up her plate of spaghetti and flung it at the bird. The pasta dish hit the same unfortunate server in the face. He backpedaled, trying to keep his balance. The big platter of food dishes wobbled more. The man backed into a table. The big platter stopped wobbling.

P'Nut ran across the first table and jumped. He twisted in mid-air to avoid some sauce that had been splattered into the air. P'Nut heard Bond's voice pierce through the noise and chaos. "My enemies will probably learn you are helping me. Be on the watch for them."

The little squirrel had jumped for the table the waiter leaned on. That table tipped. P'Nut landed and ran across the moving tabletop. The waiter fell. The big platter flew across another table, spewing food on a group of teenage boys.

The teenagers jumped to their feet and screamed what sounded like a joyous yell. "Food fight."

Screams, food, plates, birds, and glasses filled the air. P'Nut dodged flying food, water, sauces, and found a path through the flying dishes, chaos, and away from the weasels. Mr. Bond's words about his enemy knowing P'Nut helped him brought back the words about the man's friend. Mr. Bond's enemies had killed his friend. *I really don't want to die.* P'Nut raced out of the room and into the kitchen. People worked at stoves and counters. None of them noticed him. Many were gathering at the door to stare at the chaos in the dining area.

P'Nut noticed one man's white jacket had a sleeve that was near a flame and smoke rose from the edge of the sleeve. The little squirrel jumped up by him and yelled. "Your jacket is on fire."

The man looked at his smoking sleeve and quickly dunked it in a sink filled with water.

P'Nut stopped and checked his own jacket. Carefully, he brushed at a spot.

Satisfied his jacket had survived, P'Nut jumped down and raced along the floor, until he spotted the back door. P'Nut hurried over and asked a woman with a hairnet over her hair, "I need out. I need out. Please, open this door for me?"

The big lady looked down at him. "What are you doing back here? Aren't you the little squirrel doing the James Blonde imitations? Tell you what. If you do one of your imitations, I'll let you out the door."

P'Nut just wanted to get outside. *I'll just do the same one I did in there.* Trying to be patient and get it right, the little squirrel leaned against the wall and said, "The name is Blonde, James Blonde." At the same time the words of Mr. Bond echoed through his mind. "I did have a very trustworthy helper. She was my friend, at least how I understand the concept of a friend. She died. The people trying to get the crystal killed her. Please, you have to help. Don't let her life be given in vain."

I'm his helper now. They killed his last helper. Do I really want to do this? It's fun pretending to be James Blonde, but do I really want that danger?

The big lady with the hair net laughed and said, "You cute little thing. I like you." With one hand, she opened the door. "Good luck, Double oh seven. Beat the bad guys again. We need heroes like you."

P'Nut paused. "Thank you." He wanted to go, but a question came to mind. The nuts had come from here, so maybe she knew.

"How do nuts get into a jar?"

The lady just looked at him with a blank expression and slightly open mouth.

P'Nut shrugged and raced outside. Immediately, he saw the delivery truck. A man walked away from it with boxes stacked on a hand truck. He had left the back door of the truck open.

The little squirrel checked for danger. Not seeing any potential problems, P'Nut ran for the truck. He did hear a strange, quiet buzzing sound. He jumped up on the back. A metallic click came from the roof. P'Nut raced around the many boxes of fruits and vegetables. "Where should I hide?" *Did I hear something outside? What was it?* Many of the boxes had holes in them. *I could be seen too easily in them.* One box didn't have any holes, just very small cracks. P'Nut peeked through a crack. This box had enough room. The room in the box wasn't much. This time, P'Nut vibrated even more carefully. Once in the box, he settled down to wait.

After all his running and what he'd eaten, the little squirrel started to get sleepy. A noise made him lift his head, bumping it against the top of the box. The voice of a weasel came from somewhere. It sent a chill down his spine.

"I smell him in this truck."

P'Nut heard the noises of the three hunters jumping into the truck. Next, he smelled them. *I'm so glad I didn't pick one of the boxes with holes.*

His relief didn't last long.

"He went this way."

A weasel spoke from just outside of his box. "Well, well, well, what do we have here?"

P'Nut heard a weasel start biting and tearing at the edge of the box. P'Nut squirmed around just in time to see a hole growing. *I'll have to vibrate down out of the truck.* Momentarily, he thought of the strange man and his request. *I won't be able to do what Bond asked.* At the idea of not doing the mission, P'Nut felt relief and, surprisingly, some disappointment. *I hope someone else can keep that purple crystal from the bad people.* Another idea struck him. *Maybe I could use the cufflinks to chase them off.* Just before he decided what to do, another weasel spoke and the biting and tearing stopped.

"Wait, he's just going to do that trick of his. We need to plan this more carefully. We should contact our new boss."

The noises stopped, and P'Nut relaxed. His relaxation only lasted for a moment. *New boss? Who's that? What are they doing?* P'Nut didn't know. Anxiety and nervousness wouldn't let him relax. Eyes wide open, P'Nut watched, smelled, and listened. Finally, exhaustion claimed him.

The back door of the truck slamming shut briefly woke him up. The truck started with a roar. It started moving. P'Nut slipped back to sleep. He woke up to a lack of movement and noise. He smelled. The weasels were still in the truck, but they weren't close by. Those creatures were crazy. Just thinking of them made his anxiety come back. P'Nut thought of the fictional spy Blonde. *What would he do?* The little squirrel went over the next steps in his head and remembered what the pictures had looked like.

Noises and talking interrupted his thoughts. "How many of these boxes go in?"

"All of them. There was some trouble at the last delivery site. It made me late. Thanks for the help."

"We've been waiting for this shipment. We still have some trolleys to get ready."

P'Nut felt his box lifted. He patiently waited. Carefully, he looked

95

out the small hole. They entered a building with bright lights, and P'Nut smelled food. Some of the odors smelled familiar, but others were strange. He saw lots of metal. Then the box dropped onto the floor.

Looking out the hole, P'Nut recognized the place from the man's pictures. A person pushed one of those metal trolleys through a door way. A blast of cold air flowed across the floor.

When the person left the cold room and walked away, P'Nut vibrated out of his box. He could smell the weasels close by. They had followed him. Fear made him race at the door. He jumped and vibrated through it. Inside, the cold hit him. *I hope I don't have to wait in here for a long time.* He scampered around until he spotted the right trolley. Following the instructions he'd been given, P'Nut vibrated into the bottom of the trolley and curled up into a tight ball. Soon, he slept.

Movement of the trolley woke him. P'Nut remembered what he'd been told. They were taking him to an airplane. *What's an airplane? Bond should've told me what an airplane is.* P'Nut remembered his instructions and waited. He took a sniff of the air, curious if he would recognize anything. Shock and terror pushed P'Nut up off the bottom of the trolley. The odor smelled too strong. They had to be very close. The little squirrel twisted around until he looked through a narrow crack. An eye of one of the evil weasels stared back up at him.

P'Nut jerked his head back, hitting the top of the container. He froze. One of his instructions had been to be quiet. *How had the weasel gotten under him? It doesn't matter. I have to deal with this current situation.* P'Nut remembered the next instructions. He was to ignore all the movements. *For now, I'll ignore that weasel.* After Bond contacted him, P'Nut would use his vibrate ability and go through the bottom of the trolley and start causing chaos in the plane.

What am I going to do? I can't vibrate through living things.

96

Chapter Ten

Into the Mountains

Dogs have been bred to do and be many different things. Each breed is different, and some of them are very different from each other. Training makes a big difference for any dog, but just like a miniature horse cannot be trained to be a race horse, a Chihuahua cannot be trained to be a sled dog. Every breed has its built-in advantages and limitations. People are that way also.

*Newfies are loving dogs. They are also called Newfoundland dogs or Newfoundlanders. The breed originated in Newfoundland, Canada. They were originally bred and used as working dogs for fishermen, and as a result, they want to please, to help, and to save people. They **do not** like seeing people in the water. Newfies are afraid the people are going to drown, and they want to drag the people out of the water. Do not take a newfie to a pool party.*

Annie looked at Izzy in concern. "Are you okay?"

Izzy's face had turned pale after her last maneuver.

The young woman shook her head. "I will be. I'll just avoid doing any more flips. Come closer, so I can hold onto you. I think that helps."

The big newfie obliged, quickly, moving closer until Izzy threw her arm around her.

Izzy said, "Okay, let's try moving faster."

Slowly, they picked up speed. Every now and then, Annie lifted them a little higher to go over something. The higher they went, the more turbulence Annie felt from the air.

Below them, the golden fields of grain rippled from the growing wind. Their shadows raced over those fields. The shadows of growing tall, cumulous clouds drifted below them too. Those shadows deepened, as the clouds darkened.

The young woman said, "My stomach is okay with this. I just wish it was smoother. I think we have a long way to go. I'm going to shut my eyes. I'll trust you to take us to the river."

Annie said, "You're doing great. I like just moving through the air. I like it when the wind blows through my open mouth. I'll start moving more air with us. We won't feel the wonderful wind, but the turbulence won't be as bad."

Izzy said, "I'm trying. It helped to float near the ground. I still don't think I can deal with having my eyes open as we go higher."

A piercing scream rent the air. "This is my territory. Leave my territory or face my wrath."

Annie responded to the raptor's threat. "It's okay. We're just passing through."

The raptor screamed, "Your words are empty. I demand you leave."

She told Izzy, "I'm going to have to pick up our speed or get in a fight. I don't like conflict."

Izzy snorted. "You... not liking conflict? I never would've guessed. I'm just surprised you aren't making a friend of this raptor."

Annie said, "I've tried. Raptors are very problematic. Some express interest, but they— woops." Annie spotted the second raptor just in time to avoid its attack. They dodged to the side.

At the maneuver, Izzy tightened her hold on Annie. "That maneuver was still a little more than I can deal with. Can't you use gravity on them? Surely, you could stop them from attacking."

"Yes. But I don't like moving others without their permission. The only way to stop a raptor from attacking would be to force it to land. I might hurt it. I don't like taking a chance of hurting anyone."

Another shrill scream came from behind them. "Fly away and don't come back."

Annie said, "We're getting close to the river."

The rolling hills covered in fields had a scar. A river had slashed through the hills leaving behind jagged edges. At those edges, water had left behind the evidence of centuries of the water's erosion. Steep cuts, draws, plunged down into the scar, revealing basalt cliffs and feeding the seasonal moisture into the river at the bottom of the scar. This time of the year, only occasional thunderstorms provided new moisture. The building cumulous clouds hadn't caught Annie's attention. Still under a year-old, she hadn't experienced a thunderstorm. Even with more air moving with them, they still felt some turbulence, and it grew worse.

"I'm bringing us down. Izzy, do you still have your eyes shut?"

~**********~

Getting tired of keeping her eyes shut, Izzy peeked. What she saw made her open her eyes wider. The sky was filled with dark, towering clouds. "I'm looking. I think we're going to have a storm."

Along the horizon, a mountain range rose above the hills. *Why do they look so threatening?* The hills were dark with the occasional

99

bright green from sunlight peeking through the gathering storm. Even darker clouds gathered over the mountains, and as she looked, a flash of light testified to a lightning strike in those distant mountains. *I'm so glad we're not there.* A gust of turbulence struck them, and Izzy gulped. "I'm ready to go down. The sooner we get down to the river, the better."

The fields cloaking the rolling hills around them were dabbled with bright sunshine and cloud shadows. Izzy's view changed as they dropped below the crest of a basalt cliff slashed by ravines. Steadfastly, Izzy kept her gaze pointed ahead and not down.

They dropped lower and lower. Izzy wiped the sweat from her forehead. Again and again, a gust caught them. They passed the tops of some willows growing along the banks of the slow-moving river. In the distance, Izzy saw a dam.

This time, as they came down to land, Izzy remembered the first landing on the dusty dirt road, and she braced for the landing. Their feet came down gently on the rocky shore. "Annie, how did you land so nicely?"

"Last time, you were crushing me, and I was worried about you. Also, that time, you said to be quick, so I wasn't very careful."

Izzy stumbled over the rocks to the water.

Annie ran ahead of her and waded out into the water. Before Annie started drinking, she positioned herself between Izzy and the deeper water.

Izzy knelt and washed her face in the water. The water felt wonderfully cool after the hot day. She waded out by Annie.

The newfie stopped drinking and looked at her. "You aren't going any deeper? Can you swim? You know water can be dangerous?"

Izzy shuddered. "Yes, I know water can be dangerous. I used to swim, but I had an accident and almost drowned. I'm not going any deeper than this."

Annie instantly crowded against her and started pushing her back toward the shore. "That goes to prove my point. Water's dangerous. Let's get you out of the water."

Izzy laughed before replying. She started stumbling backward from the dog's pressure. "Water isn't dangerous. It—"

One of her feet twisted under her and, waving her arms in a desperate battle against gravity, Izzy fell. She expected to land with a splash, but instead, Izzy felt a lurch in her stomach.

Izzy floated two feet above the water. She was above most of the water. Other water floated in wobbling balls around her. Izzy poked one of the balls, and it wobbled away from her. The poke also caused it to lose a small amount of water in the form of a few new and very small balls. Izzy looked down at a very attentive, and she thought concerned, Annie.

Annie asked, "Are you okay?"

Izzy laughed. "I'm fine. This is amazing. How did you get the water up here?"

"I was worried about you falling into the water, and I wasn't careful. You and some of the water ended up floating."

Izzy grinned. "There's a very smart young man, a friend of mine, Noah. He would, I mean, he will love to meet you. We're supposed to be going to find him. When we do, you should show him what you can do. He'll be amazed."

Thunder interrupted their moment.

Izzy whipped her gaze around them. She noticed the stronger breeze and the falling temperature. Izzy shivered.

Another lightning strike interrupted her gaze, her thoughts, and encouraged her growing terror. In the distance, Izzy saw a curtain of rain blocking the view behind it. "Annie, we need to get out of the weather."

Both of them soared up out of the canyon. Annie said, "On the way here, I saw a barn just over the ridge."

Light flashed, signaling a lightning strike. Thunder boomed all too soon after it.

Izzy pleaded. "Hurry, Annie. I'm scared of lightning storms."

The ground receded quickly. Izzy gasped. She tried to breathe and to not let her stomach rebel at the strange movement. Izzy shut her eyes and struggled to be calm. She felt them slowing just as fast as they had accelerated.

Annie said, "I haven't experienced a lightning storm before. I'm frightened, too. We're landing."

Izzy opened her eyes to see an old barn at the edge of a field of wheat. They landed quickly, but neither of them stumbled. Instead, they both ran into the barn as thunder boomed and rumbled over them. In the barn, they huddled together on the ground as the storm shook the old structure. The time between the lightning flashes and the thunder grew closer. A pounding sound drew near. In the next instant, the rain pounded on the side of the barn and the roof above them.

It didn't take long before the roof started leaking.

~**********~

A bodily process need had woken Annie. Sunshine from the outside cut lanes of light through the inside of the barn. Annie squirmed. Nothing moved in the barn except the motes of dust drifting in and out of the lanes of light. Annie whined. "Ohhh."

She looked down at Izzy. The girl let out a snore. Annie squirmed again. Annie badly needed to go outside. The young woman lay sleeping curled against her. *If I move, Izzy will wake up, but if I don't move soon...* An inspiration came to her.

Using gravity, Annie lifted one of the smaller pieces of junk around them and dropped it. Izzy kept sleeping. If anything, she snored louder. Annie looked for something bigger. That didn't work either. Annie whimpered. "Please wake up."

Getting very desperate, Annie lifted a whole assortment of stuff piled against the inside wall of the barn and dropped it with a crash.

Izzy stirred, but she didn't open her eyes. Another creature, a rat, ran from the pile of garbage. It ran right up to them and screamed, "Did you do that? You ruined my home."

Izzy sat bolt upright and screamed, "Aaaah! A rat!"

The rat complained, "What is it with humans?" It turned around in a circle. "Why don't you like us?"

Izzy backed up on all fours, jumped to her feet and tripped over Annie's feet trying to retreat more. She landed back on the ground, rolled over, and jumped up. She gasped out, "I'm sorry, but rats scare me."

Annie commented, "You're scared of lots of things. I'll be right back." She rolled to her feet and hurried outside. From outside of the barn, Annie heard the rest of the conversation.

"Is that why you lifted my home up into the air and dropped it?"

"No, I didn't. I'm sorry. Will you be okay?"

"Humph, I'll just have to redo everything. Just leave my home alone."

Annie returned to the partially open door just in time to meet Izzy.

Izzy asked, "Did you pick up and drop the rat's home?"

Annie sat down and looked out at the field. "Maybe. My, look how late in the morning it is. Are you hungry? I'm hungry."

"Yes. Actually, I am. I better go back in and get my backpack."

Annie followed her in. In the gloom, she barely made out the rat investigating Izzy's backpack. Izzy must've seen it.

"Hey, get away from that. It's mine."

The rat ran away. "I was just exploring it."

Izzy rushed to her backpack and checked it. "Everything seems to be okay."

Together, they left the barn. Annie said, "There's a home on the other side of this field. We could see if they would let us have some food."

Izzy said, "Okay."

Up into the air they went. This time they didn't go high. They soared over the field, just barely over the tops of the wheat. Before they got very close to the house on the other side of the field, a voice called out. "We have intruders. They're strange. We have intruders. They're flying. We have intruders. Stay away, intruders."

Annie said, "It sounds like a guard dog. They can be a problem. Let me deal with it."

They landed at the edge of the field, and Annie approached the dog by herself. The two dogs slowly approached each other sniffing and circling around. A woman and two kids came out of the house. "Hello, where did you two come from?"

The guard dog said, "They flew. This dog seems okay, but I'm bothered by how strange they are. They flew. It would be safer if they left."

The woman said, "Flew? Well, that's interesting. My name's Beth, and these are my two girls, Elizabeth and Annie. Thank you, Term. You did a good job."

Izzy said, "That's funny." She pointed at Annie and said, "Our names are Annie and Elizabeth. I go by Izzy."

"Come in. I presume your flight didn't include a meal?"

The question surprised Annie until she considered the other communications. Beth's body language spoke of a joke, but Annie also saw no indications of meanness. The realization hit even as Izzy responded. Annie started wagging her tail and grinning with her tongue hanging out. *She likes laughing and wants to laugh with us.*

Izzy answered, "Meal? Oh." She laughed.

Beth and the girls laughed. Beth said, "We have some food inside, but nothing your airline would've served. Come on in, and you can eat with us. We were just getting ready for breakfast."

Everyone laughed harder.

Annie said to the guard dog, "Your people are great. I love their humor."

The dog had only relaxed a little. "Yes, my people. I protect my people. I love them. You must be safe for them, but treat them nice. I'll protect them."

Annie went inside with the others, but the guard dog, Term, stayed outside. Annie asked Beth, "Why didn't Term come in with us?"

Beth said, "His full name is Terminator, and he does a great job, but, unlike you, he really isn't interested in being around people. He loves us and would give his life to defend us, but I hope it never comes to that."

The two little girls started petting Annie. She wiggled all over in excitement. Annie had a hard time paying attention to the conversation. *These girls are so sweet. I love little girls.*

Izzy said, "Annie doesn't like to fight, but she can do things to prevent fighting."

When she answered, Beth sounded more serious. "About that, I've heard that the government is rounding up animals and people who have the new ability to play with some of the laws of physics. It all just sounds crazy. Later, we can talk more. Right now, you look hungry. Elizabeth, set another bowl on the table. Annie, I have some dry dog food. Would you like that?"

Annie had heard "hungry" and "dog food." "Yes, moving things makes me very hungry."

One of the girls asked, "Mommy, can Annie and Izzy stay?"

Beth shook her head and pointed at a big bowl. "I want to help them, but I suspect staying here for very long is not what they want or need. Annie, put that bowl on the floor."

Even as Beth said "Annie," the dog responded, before Annie the little girl could. Annie used gravity to lift the bowl, move it, and set it on the floor. The two little girls screamed in surprise and even their mother gasped.

Beth said, "Okay, that was impressive. Remember girls, it isn't what we want, but what others need that we pay attention to."

Even as she spoke, the lady had picked up a big bag of dog food and poured a large amount into the bowl.

"Thank you," Annie said before she started gulping the food down. She hardly chewed at all. Bits of food fell out of her mouth onto the floor.

Everyone else sat down at the table, and the lady, Beth said, "Before we eat, we say grace."

Izzy said, "I like that."

The conversation got through to Annie as she inhaled the food. She paused and looked up. *What are they doing?*

Beth nodded her head and said, "Let's bow our heads." As everyone did, Beth said, "Our dear, heavenly Father, we thank Thee for this food and ask for thy blessing on it. We also ask for wisdom to deal with the new and old struggles in life in the right way as children of thine. Amen."

Annie, the dog, asked, "What was that?"

Beth answered, "We gave thanks to our Father and God for this food and asked for His blessing on it."

This just puzzled Annie more. She asked, "Should I have waited before I started eating? I'm sorry. I've never heard of this god before. What is this god?"

Before anyone else could answer, the two little girls volunteered answers.

"God made us."

"God loves us."

"God is love."

"He is everywhere."

Beth interjected, "Okay, girls, thanks for your help. Annie, you're a first for me. I've never tried to explain God to an animal. Is this confusing to you?"

Annie answered, "Yes, but it's interesting. I like love." She looked back at her food. "Is it okay if I finish eating?"

Izzy answered, "Yes, Annie, you should eat. Later, if you want, I can talk to you about God."

Beth said, "Girls, pass the food to Izzy first. I think she needs to eat. I don't know, but I suspect she will need to go soon."

Izzy said, "Thanks." She started helping herself to the food. "You're right. There are people who will probably be after me and Annie. They want to study Annie, and they are bad people."

Beth rose from the table. "I saw you have a pack. I will get some more food ready for you. Is there anything else you could use? Don't be shy. I want to help."

Izzy nodded her head and spoke around the spoonful of food she'd already shoveled into her mouth. "Water, soap, washrag, a roll of toilet paper, clean underwear, and socks would be wonderful. Oh, it was very cold last night. A sleeping bag if you have one I could borrow would be amazing, but, to be honest, I don't know when or if I'll be able to get it back to you."

The lady said, "You eat, and I'll get those things ready." She paused and looked at Annie, the dog. "Will this extra stuff cause a problem for you when you fly?"

Annie swallowed her last bite of food. "No. Those things are light."

Annie finished eating and had a drink. She went outside, and the girls followed. Both of them petted her and talked to her.

Elizabeth said, "I wish you could stay. We like Term, but he doesn't like playing with us or getting petted."

Term must've heard because he answered from where he lay. "Work is serious. Safety is serious. I must protect this home."

Annie answered him, "I understand, Term. I take my work very seriously, too, but I find that humans need love, too. Protecting them is more than just protecting them from hurt. Protecting is also loving them. Girl's, I think all of us dogs have places that itch. You could ask Term where his itchy places are and scratch them for him."

Term stood up and shook himself. "That is a good idea, Annie. You are a good dog. I'll try to do this other part of protecting, too. Elizabeth, I itch between my legs and my chest."

Elizabeth ran over to him. "Okay, Terminator. Prepare to be scratched."

The door banged as Beth and Izzy left the house. Izzy's backpack looked much fuller, and she carried a bag also. "Annie, we should go. The NGO people are probably going to be looking for us. I don't want them to find us here."

"Okay. Bye, everyone," Annie said. She looked back at Term. He wouldn't be great at protecting their feelings and helping them to be happy, but he would be better. *How would I do against a threat? I don't like fighting. Could I learn to fight?*

She and Izzy lifted gently off the ground and started moving out away from the house and over the field.

"Bye."

"Bye. Good luck."

The farewells followed them out over the field. Annie gently brought Izzy closer to her. "How are you doing?"

Izzy said, "I'm actually feeling pretty good. I never thought I would get over my fear of heights, but with your help, I'm doing better. It helps that there isn't any turbulence today."

"Good. Are we going in the right direction?" Annie added, "You don't have to carry that bag."

Izzy laughed. "I thought it felt pretty light." It took Izzy a moment to pull out the round device the agent had given her. Finally, after looking at it, she pointed south toward the mountains. "Keep going toward the mountains. I think we have a long way to go."

At those words, Izzy remembered the agent's words of warning about the mountains and especially the wilderness areas. *What would happen to us if we have to land in them?*

Chapter Eleven

A False Friend

Sometimes the weirdest of things happens. Have you heard of fish working with octopus to capture fish or fishermen working with dolphins to capture fish? Coyotes and badgers hunt together and show affection-appreciation toward each other. There is so much we don't know about interspecies cooperation and friendships. How much do we not know and how weird could it get?

Coyotes are common in Native American folklore. The coyotes are a trickster character, a cultural hero, and other complex characters in those stories. All cultures use stories to teach and to entertain.

Pooh looked at the coyote and back at his dad. His dad just nodded his head. *It's my decision.* "I'll go with you."

The coyote turned and started toward the other end of the pond. "Good. I'll meet you on the trail past this pond."

Pooh said, "Okay." He turned to his dad. *I don't want to leave Dad. What did the coyote mean by it's dangerous for humans to be up here? I can't wait to get to know my new friend.*

His dad held his arms wide. "I want a bear hug before you go."

Pooh rushed to him and grabbed him in a big hug. "Dad, what

did the coyote mean by it being dangerous for you?"

"Many of the wild animals up here can do different things like the deer and pikas. If I'm careful, I'll be fine. Just remember the lessons we taught you. We tried to prepare you for your life in the wild, but somethings, like the crazy things other animals have learned to do, you're going to have to figure out on your own. I have confidence you can do this. Pooh, you're squeezing a bit hard."

Pooh released him. "Dad, you have tears. Did I hurt you?"

"No." His dad held his hand over his heart. He smiled a sad smile. "I just hurt in here. We taught you all we could, but I'm worried it wasn't enough. I hope you understand. You're a wild animal, and you should be able to live your life up here."

A leaf drifted through the air. Pooh jumped and with a snap he caught it in his mouth. "I got it, Dad."

Another leaf drifted by. The little bear ran after it. "Bye, Dad."

Faintly, from behind, he heard his dad say, "Bye, you silly old bear."

Pooh ran in spurts. At times, he had to come back to the trail. *There are so many new things to see in the mountains. The air smells so much fresher up here.* A gentle roar from the small stream caught his attention. Below him, the water of the small river rushed and splashed between and over boulders. An unfamiliar insect interrupted his contemplation of the stream. Pooh chased after it. A smell caught his attention. It smelled like... The little bear tried to remember.

A voice surprised him. "Hello, Pooh."

"Hello, Coyote. Where are you?" *That smell. It's the coyote's smell. I smelled it all the way up the hike.* Pooh lifted his nose to smell and turned his head looking where he thought the voice and smell came from. There wasn't anyone there. *I can smell him, but he isn't there.* Down on the ground, Pooh saw a strange shadow. *There's something there.*

The air shimmered and Coyote appeared. "That's what I can do. I can make light flow around me instead of reflecting back. It comes in handy at times. I'm showing you this now, so you don't act surprised if some wolves show up, and I disappear. Can you do anything special?"

Pooh thought about the question. "I can smell things really good. I knew where you were before I could see you." *Making light flow around me would be cool. How would I do that?*

"Ha. That isn't special. Let's hope there's more to you than meets the nose."

The little bear scratched his head at the saying. "Isn't it supposed to be 'than meets the eye?'"

"Yeah, but your nose is special. Speaking of which, if you smell wolves, let me know. Okay?"

"What do they smell like?"

"Like me, except stronger. Let's get going." Coyote lopped up the trail.

Pooh followed along. He switched between walking and running. They traveled through the alternating shade of tall trees and bars of sunshine. "Coyote, what's it like up at Aneroid?"

Coyote didn't say anything, and just when Pooh had decided to repeat his question, Coyote finally answered, "It's a beautiful mountain lake. And..."

The little bear waited for him to continue. A fly buzzed at him, and Pooh swatted it.

"Well, I think you'll just have to find out, but I think you'll like it. Hopefully, you can get past the wolves."

Those words tantalized the little bear's imagination. Pooh followed closer to Coyote. *Together, we can get past the wolves. That's what Coyote said earlier.*

A butterfly danced by. An annoying fly bit Pooh on his face. The little bear shook his head and swatted at it. He was falling behind. A new smell, similar to the coyote but stronger, caught his attention.

Pooh lifted his nose to get a better whiff. *What's this?* He remembered Coyote's warning. The little bear hurried to catch up. "Coyote, there's a wolf nearby."

Coyote disappeared.

I wish I could do something special like that or floating like the fish or running fast like the deer. What would the right thing be for this situation? Pooh continued on. He could still smell Coyote in front of him. There was a funny small shadow, too. At the same time, the smell of the wolf grew stronger.

A new feeling trickled up his spine. Pooh felt his hair standing up. He tried to see through the trees. His nose told him the wolf had to be over in or beyond the trees just ahead. *Is that something gray moving?*

Pooh looked at the trees around him. *I could climb up to safety.* Another thought interfered with the first. *Coyote said we would help each other to be safe. I need to stay with him. How can I help him? Coyote also said the wolves would love to eat me.* Pooh thought of his mother and father. *I don't like this adventure. The wolf smell is stronger.*

Pooh felt like crying. *Just this morning, I was safe. I only worried about eating.* At that thought, his stomach grumbled. *Stop grumbling. It's your fault.* The smell of a late season strawberry caught Pooh's attention. He was halfway toward eating it when he heard an urgent whisper.

Coyote whispered. "What are you doing?"

Standing up straight and trying to walk at the same time, Pooh stumbled and almost fell. Embarrassment kept him from answering.

Pooh remembered Coyote saying the wolves would love to eat a young bear like him. The gentle wind shifted, and the little bear lost the wolf smell.

The little bear paused. *Where did the smell come from? It has to be close. Could it be sneaking up behind me?* Pooh glanced behind him. The path was empty. Shafts of sunlight brightened the shadowy forest.

Pooh turned back. His eyes opened wide. *Where's Coyote?* From the empty trail, Pooh heard a whisper. At the whisper, Pooh almost screamed.

Coyote whispered. "There's just one. We should be safe. It might try to threaten you, but between us, we'll be okay."

Pooh's heartrate slowed, and he sighed in relief. *That's right. Coyote can disappear.* With newfound confidence, Pooh considered shouting out at the wolf. *I'll let it know I'm not afraid of it. What should I shout?*

Again, the whisper came. It came with a threat of danger and uncertainty. "Uh, oh, this could be bad. It's Lightning."

Lightning? Pooh knew about lightning. It was brilliant white light in storms followed by loud noise. *Why is the wolf called lightning?*

Again, Coyote whispered. "You'll have to rush him. He can't see me, but he could hit you with lightning. Moving will keep you safer. Good luck. Just follow this path to the lake. You can't miss it."

What should I do? What's Coyote going to do? At that, Pooh remembered seeing a tree that had been hit by lightning. His instinct to just climb a tree warred with the memory of the tree. *I wouldn't be safe.*

Pooh asked, "What are you going to do?"

This time Coyote didn't whisper. A sense of urgency filled his voice. "I can feel static electricity building. You might be too late. Go."

Pooh saw a gray form, moving in the trees. Pooh started running. He yelled, "I'm a black bear, and you're in trouble." It didn't sound like a very good threat, but it was the best Pooh could think of on such short notice.

The wolf spoke. "I hear you running, Coyote. You can't stay invisible for long. This time, we'll get you. This black bear isn't going to distract us."

We? Coyote only thought there was one. Pooh ran into the trees. From behind him came a flash of light and a boom of thunder. *That wasn't as bad as normal lightning. If only I could do lightning. This wolf and the other one would get scared.*

Coyote must've run around the trees. From the other side of the gray wolf, Pooh heard Coyote yell.

"There's another wolf. Run for your life, Pooh."

Coyote is my friend. The wolf said they would get him. The poor little bear didn't know what to do.

What can I do? Running away didn't feel right to him. Pooh continued yelling. This time, he yelled. "They will feel our stings." *Was that better? I don't like this. There's no time to think.*

The closer wolf said, "Coyote, this time, you aren't going to fool us into chasing another animal. We're going to get you."

How would it feel to do lightning? As Pooh thought about the idea he felt his fur stood on end. For some reason, his feet hadn't turned him around to run him away to safety. His stupid stomach growled, and Pooh found himself yelling again. "I'm hungry."

Pooh saw the wolf snarling as it ran. *What are the wolves doing?* Another gray shadow moved farther away. *I'm running the wrong way. Coyote said to run for my life.*

Another threat burst from the little black bear cub. This one he yelled with all the force he could muster. "Use lightning to hit us. I'll hit you with lightning."

In accent to this threat, Pooh snarled as fiercely as he could. A bright light flashed. Thunder boomed. A tree between Pooh and the wolf exploded.

The explosion knocked Pooh off his paws. The little bear shook his head to get rid of the ringing. *What's Coyote saying?*

"Pooh, you were supposed to wait until both wolves were closer. Now, they're going to get away. You ruined our plan."

One of the wolves snarled a threat. "This isn't over. We will get you for this. Next time, we'll have another pack with us. We'll have too many for this bear to deal with. He'll be like the last victim you ran from, and this time, Coyote, you will die."

Pooh blinked, trying to see.

The wolf closest to him limped away on just three legs. Its other leg seemed to be hurt. The second wolf moved with the injured one out of sight. *What happened? We didn't have a plan. What did the wolf mean about the last victim you ran from?*

Coyote blinked back into view as he jumped over the remains of the blasted tree. "Kid, you were awesome. I thought you said you couldn't do anything special, except for your special sense of smell that is. Why didn't you tell me you could do lightning? We are definitely going to be friends."

"What? I didn't do anything."

Coyote said, "You created lightning."

Pooh scratched his head, stood on his wobble legs, and said, "I don't think so. What plan did we have? I didn't know we had a plan." *Going to be friends? I thought we were friends. What were the wolves talking about?* Pooh wanted some time to sit and think everything over.

"First, about the plan I mentioned. Of course we didn't have a plan, but the wolves didn't know that. I wanted to scare them. It worked. Second, Lightning didn't make that last lightning strike happen. I've messed with him before. He can't do lightning again that quickly. That had to be you. You're a natural at survival. The first rule of survival is to never be totally honest."

"Oh." Pooh sat back down. "I didn't mean to do the lightning. I did think of how it would be to do it, but I don't think I did it." *What's going on? Coyote has to be my friend.* Even in his own thoughts, Pooh wasn't so sure anymore.

"Kid, I heard you say 'I'll hit you with lightning.'"

"I'm not good at thinking fast. I tried to come up with a scary sounding threat."

"Kid, you're a puzzle, but a good one. If you're up to it, we should get going. As much fun as it would be to see you mess with two packs of wolves, I'm feeling generous towards them. I think we shouldn't wait for them."

The little bear hurriedly got up. "I can go. Lead the way."

"You're a tough little guy."

Together, they went back to the trail. Coyote went back to his loping up the trail, and Pooh followed the best he could. At times, he limped. He tried dropping to all fours and not using his injured right front paw. That didn't work any better. *How did the wolf manage?* Pooh decided to go back to standing on his two hind feet. They were getting sore.

Pooh didn't like the rockiness of the trail. Coyote was getting far ahead. The little bear wanted to rest. Pooh opened his mouth to call out for a break. Before he could, he remembered how Coyote had called him 'a tough little guy.' Pooh liked that memory.

It didn't help Pooh that his stomach kept trying to make him stop at tasty-looking plants. *I'm hungry.* Pooh kept his eyes on the trail ahead of his paws. *I'm a tough little guy. I can do this.* His stomach disagreed. The little bear ignored it. *My stomach gets me in trouble and slows me down.* A different smell broke Pooh out of his concentration. The air smelled less dusty, and it smelled of marshes. *I don't hear the rushing of the stream.* He smelled the musky smell of the playing animal. He no longer walked on a steep path.

Pooh looked around. He walked through a meadow. Lots of tasty food grew here. Pooh looked back the way he'd come. Behind him, the trail came out of taller trees. A new voice caught his attention. Pooh turned around. Coyote stood by a pond. He seemed to be talking to someone.

The little bear heard a new animal talking. *It's the one I smell.* "I still can't believe you made it back. Who did you talk into travelling with you this time? Are the wolves eating them, too?"

Pooh slowed, puzzling over what he'd heard.

Coyote said, "I really thought the skunk would be safe. Who would've thought wolves would attack a skunk."

"They were probably just mad they couldn't catch you."

"Well, you know how it is in the mountains. It's survival of the smartest."

Another creature swam up close to them. "Well, if it isn't Coyote. Are you still tricking people and pretending to be a friend?"

The other creature spotted Pooh at that moment. "Hey, there, I haven't met you before."

Pooh said, "Hi, I'm Pooh. What are you? I've never met any animals that look like you two." The little bear paused for just a moment and then added, "Coyote is helping me get to Aneroid Lake." Even as Pooh mentioned Coyote helping him, something about it made him feel foolish.

The creature said, "I'm an otter. This is my friend, Stump. He's a beaver, and Coyote's interesting for sure, but he never helps anyone."

"I helped that rabbit."

"You tricked that rabbit, and then you ate it."

"I thought it was his cousin."

Pooh tried to take it all in. His feeling of foolishness helped. *He tricked me.* The little bear looked at Coyote. "At the pond, you told me we were friends."

Coyote said, "No. I said I can be your friend. You see, friend is an interesting concept and dangerous. It's much safer to keep friendship a safe distance away just like I did. I didn't say I was or I would be your friend. See, I kept us safe."

The little bear just stared at him. *Coyote lied to me. Except, I do remember him saying "can be." He also told the truth about the wolves wanting to eat me.*

Coyote said, "Bye. I'm heading to the meeting." The coyote trotted off down the trail.

Pooh didn't know what to do. He remembered something else, and he yelled after Coyote, "You called me friend."

Coyote called back, "So, you caught me in a lie. Big deal. See you later."

The otter asked, "What are you going to do now?"

Pooh shrugged. "I was going to Aneroid."

Stump said, "We're going there."

The little bear looked at the two smaller creatures. "Why are you going there?"

"We're going to the meeting."

"Meeting? What's that?"

"Come on. We should get going. It's at the tree. Everyone's invited. Owl has the meeting the last evening before the full moon. The meeting is where we decide on things that affect us all."

Head swirling with the conversation and badly wanting to sit down and think, Pooh followed along with them. *Meeting? What's that?*

The otter said, "Like you beavers making bigger dams."

"I don't see the problem."

A new voice interrupted, "You're flooding our homes."

Another one said, "You're a new bear. Do you know there's no hunting allowed in the meadows, this trail, and around Aneroid after noon today until moonset tonight? It is part of the Meeting Agreement. Behave yourself or face the discipline of our community."

The otter said, "She's right. I presume Coyote probably didn't tell you about all of this."

In confusion, Pooh looked around at all the new animals. More animals appeared out of groups of trees and ran out of the meadows. They all seemed to be heading down the trail toward Aneroid Lake. "No, he didn't. I've never hunted. I won't hunt today either."

The animals he walked with passed through another small group of trees. Something in the distance caught his eye, but Pooh couldn't see it clearly enough. It was something fuzzy and green sticking up in the distance. This wasn't what he'd expected. *What did I expect?*

The numbers of animals increased the farther they went. Birds flew overhead. They all climbed a slight rise, and Pooh saw a lake below them.

The otter said, "This is Aneroid Lake."

Something huge and green loomed over the far end of the lake. Pooh pointed at it. "What's that?"

Stump the beaver said, "That's the tree, and none of my people are allowed to cut any of it down." In an afterthought, he added, "You can probably find a really good place for your winter den in one of its caves. That's if you don't decide to slide down our newest project. It's warmer down by the big lake."

Pooh's mouth dropped open at the idea of a tree that gigantic. *Slide down? Big lake? What's he talking about?* The closer they got, the better Pooh could see an incredible edifice. Finally, they arrived at its base. Dozens of trees leaned together to make one tree.

The trunk above them looked bigger around than Farmer's whole farm. Pooh leaned his head back and looked at the branches high above them. "This is incredible."

Pooh noticed the animals had stopped. This must be where the meeting would be. "Why are we waiting?"

Stump pointed with one webbed forepaw. "See up there? We are waiting for Owl to start the meeting."

Pooh looked around in amazement at all the animals gathered in the friendly group. *This is amazing. I could have friends up here. There are lots of friendly animals to play Pooh ball with.*

The conversations around him ebbed and flowed. Pooh turned from one to another trying to follow all the conversations and failing to follow any. A new creature dove down from high above.

This one, Pooh recognized. It was a golden eagle.

The big raptor said, "Something unusual is coming, and I think there's danger for all of us. Is Coyote here?"

Pooh looked up trying to see what was coming. His sense of smell didn't help. It told him of dozens and dozens of different animals. One smell he didn't like.

The source of that smell spoke. "I'm here."

The eagle said, "Follow me this way. Everyone, as soon as Owl is awake, tell him that there might be trouble coming."

Coyote called out, "Pooh, I think all of us need your help. Come with me and Eagle."

Those were not the words the little bear expected. *What?* He wanted to ignore the statement. *I don't trust that liar.* At the same time, he wanted to try to help. Pooh felt the eyes of all the animals on him. He heard their voices and questions. Two stuck with him.

"Who is he?"

Stump said, "Coyote's a trickster, but he's the smartest of us. If he thinks you're needed, then please go with him."

Chapter Twelve

The Mission

Even without thumbs, Eastern Gray Squirrels have very dexterous front paws. Their paws can also rotate one hundred and eighty degrees. That is why they can run headfirst down a pole or a tree. Squirrels, including Eastern Gray Squirrels, have long whiskers. Those whiskers, called vibrissae, are very sensitive to touch and vibrations. They don't have those vibrissae just on their heads, but also in various places on their bodies. As they move, they are feeling everything much more acutely than we can imagine. For P'Nut and other squirrels that really helps in the dark.

Options formed in P'Nut's mind. *I could use my cool cufflinks. I could just wait and see what happens. I could vibrate through the side of this trolley. That sounded like the best idea.* He almost pushed off against the floor to go through the side. *Not yet. I've got to wait.*

One thing P'Nut knew for certain. The success of his secret mission could be threatened by taking action too soon. *This time, I will succeed. Well, I guess I sort of succeeded before.* For now, P'Nut was in a secure position. *The weasels can't get to me. Or is it woozles? Oh, that's right. Woozles are fictional, like Pooh in the story. I'll wait and make plans.*

P'Nut felt something lift him up. *I'm going to the plane.* When would Bond contact him?

Rested, P'Nut felt much better physically. He looked down below again. The weasels, at least two, were still down below. P'Nut opened his mouth to scold them. *I need to be quiet.* P'Nut shut his mouth. He fingered his new cufflinks. *I need to be quiet.*

The squirrel wriggled and carefully turned around. All around him were the noises of activity he had no ideas about. *What's going on out there? Is everything going according to the plan? What's my plan for getting past the weasels? I think I'll use the cufflinks. I want to see what they do.*

P'Nut tapped twice on a cufflink and stopped. His tail twitched back and forth. *I've got to wait.* He went back to his planning. *I'll vibrate through the side.*

He squirmed around and looked at the weasels again. An eye stared steadily back at him. P'Nut reached for the cufflink before stopping himself. *How are those weasels staying so calm and patient?*

P'Nut felt the berry in his pocket and an overwhelming urge to nibble on it rushed over him. Without thinking of the consequences, he pulled it out. *I love berries. I've got to do something. Just a nibble couldn't hurt.*

Something bumped the trolley. P'Nut looked at the small, white, round object. It didn't look dangerous. He remembered Bond's warning. "Do not eat any of part of the berry or its juice." Sadly, he put it back in his pocket.

In desperation, P'Nut thought back. *How do I calm down?* He remembered watching movies. *Stories, stories calm me down. What story can I think of?* The Winnie the Pooh movie came to his mind.

Now, he remembered the goofy, friendly, light brown bear. The Pooh in the movie wore a red shirt. *That bear is like me. He likes to wear something like humans.* P'Nut laughed to himself at the memory of Pooh eating all of Rabbit's honey. *Silly bear, you should've saved some.* P'Nut always made sure to save food for the future.

A different noise interrupted his memories. P'Nut had noticed many strange noises and had felt movement. The movements had been up and down. This time the noise grew louder, and he felt a stronger feeling of movement. *I'm going up again. What's happening?*

Another noise tried to get his attention. It sounded familiar. P'Nut bent his head toward the pin on his suit.

"Can you hear me? If you can, speak softly, and I will hear your answer." It was Bond.

"Yes, I hear you. Where are you?"

"I am not there, but I found out the weasels are now working with my enemy. They are on the plane with you. I do not know what their plan is. They might think you are after the crystal. I do not know if they got any gadgets from my enemy. Stay patient. I will let you know when to cause chaos."

"When?"

"Soon. That is all for now. You are doing well. Stay patient."

"When?" P'Nut waited for a response, but none came.

He tried to be patient, but odd noises continued outside of his hiding place. P'Nut wriggled around again and poked a claw through the hole at the weasels. One of them poked a claw back, and for a while they dueled, claw against claw.

A voice interrupted the duel. "P'Nut, commence causing chaos."

P'Nut jumped back from his duel and banged his head. "Oww! Finally. I'm so tired of being still and quiet." The little squirrel pushed off from the side and vibrated through the opposite wall of the enclosure. P'Nut took in the legs and shoes of a person standing near.

Jumping, he quickly, and not carefully in the least, grabbed ahold of one leg with his claws just long enough to hear a scream. He had to move fast. The weasels would be right behind him. P'Nut jumped clear and ran through a narrow doorway.

A long narrow aisle with rows of seats on either side greeted his view. A person sat on each seat. *So, this is what the inside of a plane looks like.* It didn't surprise him too much, but what did surprise him was the lack of screams or shouts.

P'Nut's mind raced as he tried to figure out what was wrong. *I don't like this. What should I do?*

The people closest to him had pulled their socks up over the bottom of their pants. *Something isn't right.* With the one scream he'd already caused, there should've been the beginning of the chaos he'd expected to create.

Someone pointed at him. Flashes of possible plans and options spun through P'Nut's mind. The walls were bare. Nothing hung from the ceiling. *If I could get up onto the back of the seats and on the heads, then...* A lady with another of the trolleys stood in the aisle.

The lady paused in the act of pouring a drink. *Water.*

Faster than his own thoughts, one of P'Nut's paws reached for the pill. Using both paws, he nibbled and swallowed. *I'm ready for the huckleberry to get wet.* One of the passengers pointed at him.

P'Nut noticed the hand wore a glove. Everyone seemed to be wearing gloves. No one had on a loose-fitting shirt.

"There he is."

An all too familiar voice said, "Be prepared."

This time, P'Nut quickly recognized the evil sound of the soft feminine voice.

That water is too far away. P'Nut fished the round huckleberry

127

out of his pocket. P'Nut raced at the lady standing in the aisle. He jumped.

The lady opened her mouth. Her hand holding the drink swept out flinging the contents across several rows of people.

P'Nut spit on the berry. *Now, the chaos will start.* He flung it.

The lady screamed.

P'Nut looked at the expressions of the people in the seats next to the aisle as he soared past. They didn't look like they were going crazy. *How long does it take? I thought it happened quickly.*

All of them had just finished putting something into their mouths. He turned just in time to see the evil smile of the short evil woman from the house he thought he'd gotten away from.

How did she get here? What's happening?

She held one of the weasels curled up in her lap and petted it.

Wow. Evil creatures like to get petted, and evil people can like petting other evil creatures.

This isn't working. P'Nut whipped his tail to change course. *They knew I would be here, and I would try to create chaos.*

The little squirrel smelled something horrible. He felt a stinging sensation on his back. Before darkness swept him up, he felt a hand grab him.

Voices spoke around him. P'Nut smelled something sharp and annoying. "He's coming to."

A gentle feminine voice with a nasty evilness to it said, "Hold him carefully."

A hand squeezed P'Nut. It hurt. P'Nut opened his mouth to scream, but he couldn't get any air to scream.

The evil lady said, "Don't kill him."

A gruff voice, the voice of someone else P'Nut thought he remembered, said, "I want to see his eyes pop out of his skull. Now, he's not such a tough guy."

P'Nut remembered running laps inside the bearded man's shirt. The little squirrel twisted his neck to look. The same man held him. From the bearded man's expression, he also remembered getting tortured by the little squirrel.

The pressure eased. The pain ebbed. P'Nut breathed. He looked back at the lady. "Do you expect me to talk?"

She said, "I expect you to die, but yes, first you will talk."

At her comment of "I expect you to die," P'Nut started rattling his head for thoughts, ideas, plans or anything to have some hope for a future. He couldn't reach the cufflinks to tap them.

Underneath me is the cargo hold. P'Nut had already noticed another movement of the plane. *All I need is another movement pushing me down.* P'Nut remembered how freaked out he'd been the first time he vibrated through the window.

I need to stall her. These thoughts took only a tenth of a second. The little squirrel asked, "Why didn't you go crazy?"

She snorted. "Our new employer told us about others who might be allied with you. They used the huckleberry trick. We were prepared."

She smiled, "Oh, your boss tried to contact you. I told him you were dead."

At that moment, Bond's voice spoke from the device on P'Nut's suit. "P'Nut, are you okay?"

"I'm in a jar."

"How did you get into a jar?"

"No, not literally, but like nuts."

The evil lady laughed at the crazy conversation.

Bond asked, "What?"

"I'm in a jam. I've been captured just like nuts in a jar."

Bond said, "None of that makes any sense. How can you be in—"

The evil lady interrupted. "That's enough of this talk. Mr. Bond, what were your plans?"

P'Nut had purposely tried to make the conversation convoluted. *I need to stall.* He knew she had asked Bond the question, but P'Nut needed more time. The little squirrel decided to do what he did best. He would just talk without any particular meaning or rattle as his old friends had called it.

P'Nut suspected that he didn't have much time to live. *This evil lady is not patient.* P'Nut interrupted. "I'm sorry. I'm sorry. What did you ask? It's hard to think while getting squeezed to death."

She said, "I was talking to Mr. Bond."

"But he doesn't know my plan. He doesn't know my plan. I would tell you everything I know, but I'm getting squeezed so hard it's very hard to remember. I—"

The evil lady interrupted P'Nut's rattling.

In an obviously fake sympathy, "I'm so sorry. Not. Mr. Bond will answer my questions, or I'll let my friend here start removing your body parts one at a time."

The weasel said, "I could take its tail off first. It's already shorter than any self-respecting squirrel would want."

P'Nut needed to stall until the plane moved again. *Everyone stares at me blankly when I ask about nuts.* "The weasel is right, but I have another question. How do nuts get into the jars?"

The lady just stared at him with a blank expression and a slightly open mouth. The weasel asked, "What?"

P'Nut felt movement. His stall had worked. It was a push down and just what he needed. "Goodbye."

He vibrated. The weasel leapt off the lady's lap. The vicious creature flew right at Pooh, but it was too late. It missed. P'Nut and the bearded man had already started to pass through the chair. The man screamed all the way down. His meaty hand immediately let go of P'Nut. Fortunately for the man, P'Nut kept ahold of him until they fell through the floor and into the darkness.

Unfortunately for the man, P'Nut was mad. The man had managed to get jammed between two containers. The man was in a bad situation.

P'Nut didn't know what would've happened to the man if he hadn't fallen all the way with P'Nut through the chair and the floor, but P'Nut didn't want to find out. After all, he was a sensitive squirrel. The idea of someone stuck halfway through some combination of a chair and a floor sounded horrible, the thing of nightmares.

The little squirrel instantly stopped vibrating and pushed away from the still screaming man the moment they had fallen clear of the floor. The man fell between the containers. P'Nut couldn't see very well in the darkness, but he felt his surroundings.

P'Nut raced about finding various shaped objects, and with the help of his whiskers, the vibrissae, P'Nut built a map in his mind of the room and the objects in it. The activity reminded him of how easy it had been to race through the tree.

The man kept screaming. He must've been terrified by falling

131

through the solid objects and landing in darkness, but he also screamed from something else.

P'Nut hadn't liked getting hurt. When he fell with the bearded man into darkness, P'Nut knew from experience that people didn't see in the dark. The horrible man was at his mercy.

P'Nut really hadn't like getting crushed in the bearded man's fist. He quickly knew where the man struggled to get out from between two containers. P'Nut needed a plan. In the meantime, he did not need the threat of the man being free. At least that was the excuse he used.

James Blonde would've knocked the man out or shot him. P'Nut couldn't knock the man out, and he didn't have a gun. *What would those things in my cufflinks do to him? I better save them.* Even if he could've used a gun, P'Nut really didn't like the idea of shooting someone.

P'Nut was not averse to biting and scratching. Moving fast as he explored, the little squirrel made sure to come back by the struggling and screaming man to bite and or scratch him every few seconds.

In his exploration, P'Nut discovered a very long room, similar to the size and shape of the room above it. The screaming stopped.

In a voice that sounded very different, the bearded man begged. "Please stop. I'm scared of the dark. You're right, my mother warned me, but I've been a very bad man. I've always picked on others smaller than me. I'm sorry. I'm so sorry. Please stop."

The plea didn't surprise P'Nut. After all, the man had begged and apologized before. This time, though, he'd made an admission of past sins. *What was his mother warning him about?* The little squirrel remembered a TV show he'd watched where a psychologist had worked with crazy people. *People are all crazy in some form. I'm crazy too.*

P'Nut stopped before attacking the man again. P'Nut asked in his

132

best psychologist voice, "Relax. Why do you pick on smaller people?"

In the darkness, the sounds of the man struggling stopped. In a calmer voice than P'Nut had heard from him, the bearded man said, "I don't know."

"Was there ever a time when you were small and someone hurt you?"

The man answered, and his voice had changed again. He sounded younger and uncertain. "No."

And then he added, "My mom always protected me."

"What did she protect you from?"

In a voice filled with agony, the bearded man said, "My dad. He often came home drunk. Mom would send me to my room and tell me to stay there. I still hear the yelling and screaming in my dreams."

P'Nut didn't know what to think or say. This story was getting terrible.

The words kept pouring out of the bearded man. Each phrase made P'Nut's heart hurt more for the little boy in the man. "One night, I couldn't stand to hear the pain in my mother's screams anymore. I came out of my room and shouted at my dad to stop. He turned around and said, 'You little runt. I'll teach you to respect me.' I could see mom's face. Dad had been hitting her again."

The man started sobbing. He only resumed speaking with difficulty. His words of pain sounded like flames dancing on wood, devouring the wood. P'Nut couldn't imagine living with such hurt and memories tearing at his internal fabric. *It would tear me apart.*

"Dad lurched at me. I couldn't move. I was terrified. Mom tackled him. She yelled at me, 'Run to the neighbors! Run!' She must've known that things would end badly for her. I'll never forget the last thing she said. 'Don't be a bad man like your father. Be good.'

She died that night, and I've failed to live up to her last request."

Silence filled the darkness around them. P'Nut thought he heard something different from outside their dark room. P'Nut said, "I'm sorry I bit and scratched you."

The bearded man said, "That's okay. You're quite the little fighter." In a surprised voice, he added, "I've never told anyone that story before, and you know what? I feel better. Is it okay if I get out of this spot? It's quite uncomfortable."

"Sure. I'll help you." P'Nut guided the man's hand to a better hold.

It didn't take long before the two of them sat silently in the darkness together.

The man broke the silence. "P'Nut, what are you going to do?"

"I don't know. I was supposed to be a hero and help keep some bad people from getting a special crystal, but everything's a mess."

At that moment, P'Nut heard Bond's voice. "P'Nut, what has happened?"

"They were ready for me. I failed to create chaos. I've managed to get down into the cargo hold. What should I do?"

After a short pause, Bond answered, "We'll have to go to our plan B. You're going to have to try to get the crystal to Noah. I don't know if you can do it. I don't think you can get the container open to get to the crystal."

The bearded man said, "I can open the container for my friend."

Bond sounded very surprised. "You have a friend with you?"

P'Nut said, "Yes, I do. He's a good man, and he likes helping other little people."

In an emotional voice, the bearded man said, "Yes, yes. Let's find the container. Which one is it?"

Bond said, "This could work. You have some time. I can make a slight adjustment to the plane's course. When you are over Noah's location, I'll let you know."

"Okay. But what if something happens here, and I can't wait to leave?"

"In a little bit, I'll start lowering the plane's altitude. That will make it easier for you to breathe outside the plane."

P'Nut didn't understand what Bond talked about. *Why would I have trouble breathing outside the plane?* The little squirrel just shrugged. There had been a lot he didn't understand. There was still the one answer he'd love to know. *How did nuts get into a jar?*

The man used the flashlight feature on his phone to provide light. Working together, P'Nut and the bearded man found the right container and removed the necklace with the crystal.

A different question had been bothering P'Nut. Why hadn't the bad guys been worried about him vibrating down into the hold? At first, he'd thought that they were too stupid to think of it, but after seeing how the crystal was stored in its container, P'Nut knew he wouldn't have been able to get it without help.

Using the phone, his friend looked at the purple crystal and said, "I wonder what the big deal is with this?"

A bang from the other end of the cargo hold made P'Nut look up. His eyes didn't see what it was in the far darkness, but his nose told him. The weasels had found their way into the cargo hold.

His friend, the man, obviously didn't have as good of a sense of smell. He turned his phone light toward the noise and said, "What was that?"

The light didn't do great at showing the far end of the hold, but P'Nut could make out the weasels running and leaping over the containers.

His friend said, "Uh oh, this is bad."

P'Nut agreed. This time, he had nowhere to run. His new friend might try to help him, but the image of the dog fighting with the weasels came to mind. Also, he relied on his phone to see. The little squirrel worried that the little weasels would terrorize his friend.

I've got to go. I wish I could communicate with Bond. The weasels moved way too fast.

His friend spoke quickly. "You need to leave. I hope you'll be okay jumping out of the plane. Maybe your trick will help." He held out the necklace and crystal. "Here. Take this."

The weasels had already closed the distance. They would be on them in seconds. *We're moving too slowly.*

P'Nut grabbed the necklace and crystal and held them tight. "Pick me up, and throw me down through the floor."

His friend picked him up.

The weasels jumped.

P'Nut tensed, ready to fight for his life. He felt something grab his tail.

Chapter Thirteen

Danger Increases

Physics, especially quantum physics, gets mind-bending-crazy, and that makes it fun. Albert Einstein referred to some of it as 'Spooky Action.' One of the theories of physics is about something called Dark Matter. This theory was created to solve a problem in another theory. In my books, Dark Matter isn't just a theory. It is a real substance, and just like other real substances, it has an effect on some living organisms. The effect of Dark Matter is very unique. It changes the minds of some organisms and allows them to play with the laws of physics. This makes for crazy, dangerous, and fun stuff, and that is just like real physics, just in another mind-bending way.

Annie said, "I'm going to pick up our speed and go higher. Are you ready?"

Izzy answered, "Move me closer, so I can put my hand on you. Touching you helps me to be calmer and not frightened."

"Done. Let's go." Annie slowly lifted them higher and increased their speed. "Are you still okay?"

Izzy said, "Stop worrying about me. If I start to have trouble, I'll let you know. Get us going faster. I'm worried about the bad guys we left behind, and I can't wait to introduce you to Noah and my other friends. I think you'll like them. I know Noah is going to have lots of questions for you. What you do with gravity's amazing."

As Izzy spoke, Annie picked up speed. The rolling hills started flying by under them. Soon, they saw between the hills occasional, narrow, green, hidden valleys. Those valleys had tall willow trees and occasionally scattered cottonwood trees. Evergreens grew scattered on the north-facing slopes of the hidden valleys. The mountains drew closer and closer. The hills rose to meet them, and Annie took them higher to get above them.

To the west, a river flowed down through a green, wider, agricultural valley. Izzy said, "That looks beautiful over there."

Happy at her comment, Annie responded, "You're doing so much better."

Izzy said, "I'm still being careful not to look straight down. It helps that you take the air around us with us. I see the ground moving past, and I don't feel any wind. I feel like I'm in a plane looking out the window."

Below them, the hills carpeted with fields had changed over to ridges serrated by steep canyons. A forest of pines covered most of the higher terrain. Annie felt Izzy not just resting a hand on her, but she had started petting her. The petting sent a shiver of pleasure through her body. "Izzy, do you have any idea how much farther we need to go?"

It took Izzy a while before she answered. "The disk shows Noah still south of us, but the direction isn't steady. I think he's moving. Let's keep going this direction for now. We must be getting closer."

After a pause, Izzy added, "I would like to get past these mountains as quickly as possible. I've heard the areas with mountains and wildernesses are dangerous."

Annie picked up more speed. "I'll do the best I can. I'll take a little less air with us. Let me know if it gets too rough. I'm still going to need rests. Going faster will wear me out sooner. What can you tell me about Noah? Is he alone or with others?"

"Noah is a young man, my age, eighteen. He's tall and has red hair. He is quiet and shy, but he loves animals, and he's a genius."

"What's a genius? The thingy by my ears isn't translating it into anything I understand."

Izzy said, "I've always wondered how those things translate everything. I guess they're limited by what you can understand. A genius is someone who's very, very smart."

Annie asked, "Do you like Noah?"

"Yes, but I got very mad at him, and even though I apologized, I'm worried he might not like me as much. The worst of it is I'm still a bit upset even though I know it isn't reasonable. It's frustrating."

Annie said, "That's funny. I think all humans are very smart. I'm surprised to hear how different some of you are and how you have trouble controlling your emotions. I'm that way also. Not about getting mad. I don't tend to get mad, but I do get excited, and when I do, I can get into trouble. I'm trying to be calmer, but it's hard. Is Noah by himself?"

Izzy answered, "I'm sorry, I get distracted talking about Noah. There are also some amazing animals with him."

They continued soaring over the forested mountains as they talked. Annie could see what looked like a big valley between the mountains they flew over and other taller mountains farther away. Annie had also noticed a roaring sound growing from behind them. She looked back. It looked like some kind of flying machine. Back where they had come from, Annie could see a column of smoke rising.

Izzy continued, "There's a big tiger. He's called Tigger. He can have anger problems, too, but he's learned to have fun. There's a little white dog named Frise. You'll like her. She thinks everyone's a friend. I think you two have a lot in common."

The young lady stopped petting Annie and pointed ahead of

them. "There's a valley ahead of us past that mountain coming up. Would you like to stop for a rest? It would be safer than resting in the mountains."

Annie responded, "I'm doing fine for now, but it would be good to stop for water and a break before long. I'm getting thirsty." She looked back again. The thing kept getting louder and closer.

Izzy said, "Okay. Also, there's a little black cat named Boots. She's a good friend, but also sneaky and likes to trick people. In other words, she's good to have on your side. There's a raven named Sally who's quite smart. A red-tailed hawk who used to think he was an eagle. He's quite fierce. There's another I can't quite remember."

Below them, they passed above the highest ridge of the mountains. It ran the same direction they flew. Off to their left, the ground dropped away to the valley. This end of the valley had patches of trees. The other end, the wider part, was mostly fields and a couple of towns. Annie said, "Should we drop lower? I see some water in the valley."

Izzy asked, "Do you see that jet coming up behind us? It seems to be getting closer." She added, "There's a smoke column behind us. I hope the people who helped us are okay."

Annie looked at the noisy thing. *Jet... I wonder what a jet is.* She asked, "What's a jet?"

"It's a plane that goes fast, and this kind is used for fighting. It seems to be slowing down and coming closer. I'm afraid they might be after us."

Annie said, "I don't like it. It's very noisy."

Izzy asked, "What?"

Annie could barely hear her. The jet kept coming closer. The dog tried moving them out of the way of the jet thing. Its noise hurt her ears. If it was for fighting, Annie didn't want anything to do with it. *I*

140

don't like anything to do with fighting.

The jet kept maneuvering with them. At times, it came closer, and, at times, Annie managed to move away. She kept going lower. If Annie had to, she would land them. *I think it's trying to force us to land. What would the jet do? What should I do?* Annie remembered the raptors. Hawks on the ground were not a problem. They could only attack from the air.

Annie heard Izzy's scream. The jet had maneuvered right in front of them. *It's getting too close. I don't know how to fight. What should I do?* Annie dropped them straight down and swerved to the side, changing directions totally. The jet couldn't keep up with that.

Annie's relief didn't last. The jet compensated and maneuvered even closer. Just like the turbulence from the storm, its exhaust buffeted them. *It's so hot.*

Only one thing to do came to her mind. Annie hated to do what she was thinking of. *I don't want to fight. I could hurt them.* Annie remembered the guard dog. I need to be more like that guard dog even if I don't like it. If we land, the jet could still attack us. Annie couldn't keep gravity moving Izzy, the bag, and the air around them, let alone herself and do this.

The bag fell. Annie fell and she pulled the jet down with her. The engine roared even louder.

It was stronger than her efforts. *I can't force it to land.* Annie saw a person in the jet. Annie remembered how she'd ruined the one car. *I could ruin this jet. I've got to let Izzy fall for a moment.* Below Annie, the ground rushed up to meet her. *I've got to hurry.* Concentrating all of her effort, the dog reversed how gravity pulled on the back, bigger part of the jet. At the same time, Annie pulled with gravity hard on the front part where the person sat. That portion ripped free from the rest of the jet. Instantly, in relief, Annie let the big noisy part of the jet go. It tumbled through the air and crashed into one of the groups of trees with a huge explosion.

Annie halted her fall and the bags. A tree top swayed beside her. She looked above for Izzy. The young lady fell toward her. Now, Annie could hear Izzy.

"Annie, help! Help me! Fuego, you can't keep me up."

Quickly, Annie cut the gravity dropping Izzy. She hadn't felt this tired in a long time. Annie moved with the bag toward Izzy. She was going to ask who Fuego was when Annie spotted a little hummingbird frantically tugging on Annie's black, frizzy hair.

The little hummingbird, in his rapid-fire voice, said, "I'm amazing. I may be small, but I'm doing it. I'm doing it. I'm saving you from falling. I won't let you die. Noah would be very upset if I did. He's been moping ever since we left you. I'm amazing. I didn't know how strong I am."

Annie heard another noise. She looked back at the man in the jet part and saw that somehow the person had left it and now floated under something white. Gladly, Annie let the jet part fall. Fatigue weighed on her bones. *I'm so tired. I don't know how much longer I can keep us flying.*

Annie said, "I don't know how much longer I can keep us flying."

Fuego asked, "Who are you? How are you flying?"

Izzy spoke up. "Annie, this is Fuego, a good friend of mine. Fuego, this is Annie a good friend of mine."

Annie said, "I—" The rest of her attempted explanation of flying got cut off by the hummingbird.

In a rapid-fire voice, Fuego said, "Nice to meet you, but you can't rest out here in the open. There are others coming."

Annie said, "There's a stream over there. Could I stop for a drink? That would help me."

The little hummingbird said, "Okay, but you'll need to get right back into the air and head for trees on the slopes ahead of us or better yet, the mountains."

The tired dog immediately dropped Izzy and everything by the water. At first, she staggered, but the idea of water lent strength to her legs. The water felt so good in her mouth. *I didn't know how thirsty I was.*

~**********~

Izzy stood, bent over, with her hands on her knees. "That was terrible back there, Annie. Thanks for saving us."

The knowledge that danger still threatened them helped Izzy recover. She got some water for herself out of her pack. She tried to grin at the sight of Fuego buzzing by some flowers along the stream. Her grin felt forced. "Are you getting much from them?"

Fuego said, "Yes. I needed to stop for food. After I fuel up, I'll go check on those others coming this way."

Izzy said, "Annie, I'll start walking. When you are ready, just pick me up."

The trees beside the stream provided some shade and better yet, they helped to hide them. The direction Izzy thought they needed to go followed the stream for a short distance and went across what looked like a pasture.

Izzy put away her water and pulled out the disk. She looked up from it and at the mountains Fuego wanted them to head for. That was the direction they needed to go. Again, Izzy remembered the agents warning about the mountains and especially the wilderness areas. *Would those animals in the mountains and wilderness areas be smarter like Annie, Fuego, and the others?* The idea of a smarter wolf sent a shiver down her back.

Would the mountains be any more dangerous than the jet or those helicopters that came toward them? Izzy had seen them before they'd landed. Those helicopters would surely come to where the jet had crashed. Izzy shifted from walking to running. At first, bushes and trees slowed her, but after climbing over a fence, running got easier.

The longer Izzy ran, the faster she went. *I can rest when Annie carries me.* In the distance, she saw some cattle. On foot slipped when Izzy stepped onto something flat, round, and brownish-green. She almost fell. Izzy staggered and brushed against a nettle. "Ouch."

The fresh cow pie made Izzy think about the cows. Thinking of them helped to distract her from the fear she ran from. *What are cattle like to talk to?* Thoughts of hamburgers and steaks came to mind. *How can I talk with what I might eat?* Izzy dodged around a tall blackberry bush. Ahead of her, she spotted some of the cattle standing in the shade of a big, wide tree. *What would I say to them? Thanks for all of the hamburgers and steaks? What would they say?*

Izzy ran past a tall bush. A loud voice distracted her. She felt something under her foot.

"Hey! Get out! Get out of my field, now!"

Izzy's head instinctually turned toward the loud voice, as she felt her foot twisting. Izzy started falling. The biggest cow she'd ever seen stared back at her.

"I said, out! Get out!"

It looks mad. Oh, it's not a cow. It's a bull. Izzy tried to roll with the fall. *I don't need a twisted ankle.* Behind it, she saw some other cows grazing.

Another voice spoke from behind Izzy.

Annie said, "Are you in danger?"

Before the bull had been loud, now, it roared. "WOLF! WOLF!"

The grazing cows lifted their heads and spun to face Izzy. The bull charged. Izzy screamed.

She left the ground just as the bull passed under her. One of its horns just missed her. The cows charged up. One said, "Call our owner, and tell him we have a wolf in the pasture."

Another of them said, "That isn't a wolf. It's a dog. Call our owner, and tell him we have a stray dog in the field."

Izzy said, "Thanks, Annie. We should leave, but keep us close to the ground. That will protect us from the helicopters seeing us."

Annie said, "I'm sorry I wasn't there sooner. That animal almost hurt you. Did you fall? Are you okay?"

"I think I'll be okay."

They flew over the ground. Alternately, they rose or fell depending on the terrain, bushes, and trees. In the more open fields, Izzy encouraged Annie to fly faster.

Behind a hill and a little way into the forest, they found a road. Annie said, "I'm too tired to fly us over this forest and the mountains. I need us to walk and run for a while. Hopefully, we can find another stream, pond, or any water would be great."

Gingerly, Izzy tried her ankle. At first it hurt some, but it felt better after walking a little on it. "This will be good. Fuego can find us easily on this road."

They made it down a straight stretch and around a bend before hearing a familiar noise.

Fuego buzzed down from his scouting. "You and Annie need to go faster. The helicopters are getting closer. Also, I saw dozens of flying things get dumped out of the helicopters. Those smaller things are flying around. I think they are looking for you and Annie. If you don't go faster, they're going to catch you."

Izzy shifted from walking to running. "I'm sorry, Fuego. Maybe you should leave us and go back to Noah and the others."

"I can't leave you. Noah would be furious with me, and I would be furious with me. I'd probably set myself on fire. Maybe I should go set the helicopters and those flying things on fire. It worked very well with the white parachute things."

Izzy said, "No. There are too many of them."

Fuego said, "Okay, but I'm not afraid of them. If they attack, they will learn to fear me. We are headed for some very tall mountains. You could hide in those mountains."

Izzy ran faster. "Yes, the shortest route is over those big mountains ahead of us." At those words, Izzy remembered again the agent's words of warning about the dangers of the mountains. *We don't have a choice.*

Fuego said, "Okay. Over these mountains we go, but if you don't move faster, they'll catch you. I'll gladly go down fighting to slow them down."

Izzy found herself running in the air and not on the ground. The road disappeared behind them. "Annie, you said you were too tired to fly us."

"I can do this. I have to."

Fuego said, "Maybe make short flights. I'll scout ahead."

Izzy pleaded, "Promise you'll try to avoid those flying things. I'm afraid this time is different from last time. This time we don't have the help of the crows."

The little hummingbird said, "I've watched the flying things.

They can't go where I can go, and I'm faster at changing direction. They will fear me."

The fearless bird zoomed away before Izzy could respond. She felt acceleration and drew nearer to Annie. They curved around trees and up a hill moving faster and faster. Izzy gasped and leaned to the side, as a large tree branch loomed in front of her. A smaller branch brushed against her leg, spinning Izzy.

She fought both her stomach and the spinning. Annie must've noticed her problem. Izzy felt a gentle tug on her leg, and the spinning slowed to a stop.

Izzy pointed. "Do you see that dirt road? It's going close to the same direction we need to go. We would be out of sight between the trees and have a clear path to follow." *Hopefully, I won't get spun again.*

Annie responded to the suggestion by shifting their course. They followed the road around hills and then down. From ahead came the sound of a stream. "Sorry I got you too close to that tree. You're right about this road. It will be safer and easier."

Izzy looked back the way they'd come. *How will Fuego find us?* A familiar buzzing sound lifted her gaze. Something moved above the road. The buzzing grew stronger. Izzy gave a sigh of relief when Fuego flew up.

"I had a hard time finding you. This is a good route. Follow this stream up into the forest. Continue the same direction, and you'll find a canyon. Get down to the bottom. It will be harder for them to see you. Down below, there's a river. Go up the stream. You should be safe. I found some tasty flowers by the stream. I filled my tank. I need fuel for a fight. I'm going back to slow down some of them. I'll meet you along that river."

Annie said, "I'm afraid we're going to have to land and run or walk. Otherwise, I'm going to fall."

147

Fuego said, "Oh, okay. I'll just slow them down more. They will fear this hummingbird."

Izzy gasped, "Oh, Fuego, be careful."

The little bird must've heard, because he answered as he buzzed away. Izzy only heard the first part. "I'm never care..."

Chapter Fourteen

Fuego's Battle

Robotics is advancing rapidly. In many countries like Japan, the births are not keeping up with deaths. The result is a big labor shortage. The solution is to increase automation. Also, with the elderly population increasing and not having enough caregivers more caregivers are needed. Robotics is providing robots for both increased automation and for caregivers. That is good. Unfortunately, as in this story and in reality, robotics is also being used to make new weapons of war. I hope that in the race for more powerful robotic weapons of war man does not create his own doom.

The ground rushed up below them. Izzy hit the ground trying to run. At first, she stumbled and almost fell. Shifting her weight, Izzy managed to shift successfully to running. "Annie, can you rest while you run?"

"Some. I'm going to the stream for a drink. It would help if you keep running to the top of the canyon."

Izzy nodded, saving her breath. *Now, I can make good use out of being a star athlete.* She'd always loved running. Falling into her old habits, she blocked why she ran. Her world narrowed to just her immediate surroundings, breathing, and running.

Trees and rocks flew by. The air felt fresher up here in the mountains. With each breath, flowing in and out, part of her tension and fear flowed out. Some of the trees had berries. One branch with

149

berries leaned down, offering the fruit to her. Izzy ducked away from the strange movement. Again, the agent's warning came back to her thoughts. *'Try to avoid spending any time in the mountains and wilderness.' The plants have been affected, too, and I'm going into mountains.*

Unfortunately, the road didn't continue in the direction she needed to go. On top of that, bushes, trees, rocks, and more branches waving their fruit in her face slowed her down.

She didn't see any animals. Her foot landed with a crunch on a dried up plant. *It wouldn't take much to start a forest fire up here.*

Izzy heard a voice from the trees. "Warning, warning a human is coming into our woods. Warning, warning a human is coming into our woods."

Izzy gasped, "I mean all of you no harm. I'm running from danger and trying to get to a friend."

~**********~

Fuego buzzed back toward their enemies. Evergreen treetops gently swayed below him. The forest stretched out in all directions. *That forest have to be full of animals. There has to be more creatures like that chipmunk down there.* His mind flitted away to the upcoming battle.

The helicopters had slowed down, but they continued moving toward the mountains. *This forest has slowed their search. I was right about sending my friends into the trees and the mountains.* Groups of smaller flying machines swooped over, between, and around the tree tops below the hummingbird.

The little machines didn't interest him. He focused on the largest challenge. From the trees below, Fuego heard a loud noise. It sounded like an explosion. Fuego normally would've investigated, but he had business to take care of.

The little hummingbird didn't think about tactics or strategy. He thought of intimidation. Fuego kicked his speed up and flew straight at the closest helicopter. If there had been a bigger enemy, he would've attacked it.

Fuego thought only like a hummingbird. He had a sword, and his enemy would feel it. The helicopter grew louder.

The little fighter didn't totally ignore reality. Part of him wanted to find a spot to ram his sword, the little bill that jutted straight out from his face. He could see the propellers chopping the air over the helicopter. *It would be bad to fly up there.* This machine is *moving slowly. They are searching for my friends. I will give them something else to think about.*

The closer Fuego got, the bigger the helicopter looked. *This thing is big and noisy. I need a big fireball.* Right before he attacked, the little hummingbird realized two people sat inside of the machine looking out at him.

A big fireball blasted out from him, engulfing the front of the helicopter. The machine tipped and turned away. The helicopter's engine roared. The machine rapidly increased its speed. It continued to tip. The helicopter also rotated, and, as it did, the helicopter dove away from him. Smoke blossomed from the top of it.

Wind from the helicopter buffeted Fuego. Fuego compensated for the turbulence. He swerved. *They are retreating.*

A trail of smoke identified the helicopter Fuego had attacked. That one flew away. The others hovered well away from where he flew. *They fear me. My friends will get away.*

Fuego slowed and circled, considering the battlefield. *I have met the enemy and won.* In the far distance, Fuego noticed dots slowly getting bigger.

A growing humming sound interrupted his victory dance. Dozens of the smaller machines flew up from the trees below him. *They are too small to carry people.*

I think they are looking to attack me, but how? They are a similar size to the hawks that attacked me, but I don't see talons or beaks. They are small and easy to avoid.

Fuego considered just ignoring them, but they wanted battle. *I will give them what they want.* He wanted to dive down at them and wildly blast them with fireballs. These things still made him think of the hawks. *Hawks are dangerous.*

Fuego fell back onto his tried-and-true philosophy. When in doubt, attack. The little hummingbird dove at the dozens of drones rising toward him.

The hummingbird kicked his speed up. More of the drones lifted from the trees. *There are a lot of them.*

It will be easy for me to hit one. They can't hide. I can't miss. This will be fun. The fearless fighter blasted off a fireball. Fuego swerved and fired off another.

The first fireball hit a rising drone. With a boom, it exploded into fragments. *What?*

The shock wave from the explosion hit Fuego. He tumbled, righted, and accelerated. The burst of speed moved him just far enough away to escape the shrapnel blasting from the explosion.

Another drone flew into the second fireball. It exploded. Instinctually, Fuego buzzed straight up. His speed dropped, but he gained distance.

This time he felt one of the fragments hit his tail. Momentarily, he tumbled again.

Below Fuego, the rest of the drones continued rising to meet him. Focusing on the highest and closest, he shifted to horizontal flight. Fuego fired off more fireballs and buzzed away.

More explosions came from behind him. This time, he had managed to gain a safe distance before they exploded.

Fuego turned in a long rising arc. He looked back at the results of his attack. Debris fell, but Fuego couldn't see any noticeable reduction in the numbers of drones. *I think there are more of them. They aren't afraid. They aren't giving up. How can I stop them?*

The brave, tiny bird noticed the drones had another strategy. The ones farther away flew straight up. *They're higher than me. They're trying to surround me.* The idea of the drones converging on him from all directions didn't scare Fuego. The idea of them exploding at close range didn't scare him.

I am Fuego. I am scared of nothing. Something did scare him. His friends would be by themselves. *My friends need me.* There was still one gap. The little hummingbird blasted at his best speed back toward the helicopters. Instinctually, Fuego knew that the people in those machines worked with the drones and would be frightened by drones exploding too close to them.

In front of Fuego, drones accelerated to fill the gap. He pushed his speed to its limits. Fuego fired off a series of fireballs.

Explosions filled the air. Fuego, smoky, dazed, and with a headache, blasted through the smoke and wreckage. The headache felt familiar. In the other battle, Fuego had gotten the same kind of headache after firing off dozens of fireballs. Back then, the more he'd kept firing off fireballs the harder it got to do them. *I'm running into my limit. What am I going to do?*

The helicopters retreated faster. They flew away and toward the approaching objects. They mustn't have liked the idea of the drones exploding near them or having more fireballs blasted at them.

A quick glance back showed Fuego that the drones had broken off their attack and flew back toward the trees and the mountains.

A voice screamed from above. "Fighter, would you like some help?"

Fuego looked up. A golden eagle dove from high above him. Behind the eagle, towering clouds grew. *I didn't notice the weather changing. Can I trust this eagle, or should I blast it?* Fuego hadn't known any eagles except for the brief experience he'd had chasing Tuffy's sister, and she'd been a bald eagle.

The eagle seemed to respect the dangerous hummingbird because he broke out of his dive and soared a respectful distance from Fuego. "I'll take care of those machines."

Fuego saw the results of the eagle's words. Two of the helicopters slammed into each other. A tremendous explosion followed. Fire, smoke, more flying debris filled the air. The last remaining helicopter retreated faster.

Something far down on the ground caught Fuego's attention. Six metal-human-like things ran across the ground in a clearing.

They carried long tubes. One of them started to lift the long pointy end of the tube.

Fuego remembered the big boss shooting Star, the other red-tailed hawk. "We need to get out of here. Those metal things on the ground are going to start shooting at us."

"I don't know what shooting is, but I trust you."

The eagle turned and quickly picked up speed. Fuego accelerated faster, but the eagle caught up to him. An updraft swept both of them skyward. The eagle asked, "What are you trying to do?"

"My friends, a dog and a human, are trying to escape over those tall mountains. These machine-things are after them. Can you make those smaller drones crash into each other?"

"Sorry, my head is hurting, and when it hurts, I can't do any more of that stuff. I can show you a safe place for your friends. I have many friends who can help them."

"Okay, great. I think we have delayed those drones long enough. Let's get this information to my friends. I'll show you where they are, and you can show me where they need to go."

The eagle beat her wings, turned, and soared higher. "The updrafts are getting strong. There's going to be a lightning storm."

Fuego pushed his battered body as hard as he could, but he couldn't keep up with the eagle. Frustrated, he refused to ask for the eagle to slow down.

The eagle looked back. She said, "Can I slow down? I'm getting tired."

Grateful, Fuego gasped, "Okay. I can see over the first ridge." *I need more food. I can't keep up this hard work without more food.* A cold downdraft pushed them lower. Fuego shivered in the colder air. *I'll just have to keep going until I give them the message. They'll be so happy. They're almost safe.* They flew out of the downdraft and soared higher.

The eagle pointed out a lake and a very tall tree above it. "That's where my friends are gathered. I will inform them of your problem and come back to help you and your friends get to us."

A canyon below them caught Fuego's attention. The vegetation looked different. *That looks like a good spot for late season flowers. It's a good spot to refuel.*

The eagle asked Fuego, "Are those your friends down by the river?"

"Yes. I'll go give them the directions."

155

"I'll go alert my people. Some of them, and one in particular, are quite smart. We'll make a plan. Your friends will be safe." The eagle soared away.

A shadow moved over Fuego. He shivered more and looked up. A darker cloud grew over him. *I don't like being out in storms. This weather is looking very bad.* The cold, battered little hummingbird dove down to his friends. On his way down, Fuego studied the forest back the way he had come. He couldn't spot any of the drones or those other walking machines with guns. *I succeeded. They'll be safe. I just need to get them farther into these mountains.*

Down below him, Izzy ran along the river. Her mouth hung open, and sweat dripped off her chin. Annie floated along beside Izzy. In that brief moment, Izzy stumbled and barely caught herself. As Fuego dropped lower, he could tell by the torn jeans and bloody knee that Izzy hadn't caught herself at least once.

The air down in the canyon felt wonderfully warm. Fuego buzzed down. "Annie, you two need to get out of this canyon and over that next ridge."

Immediately, Izzy lifted off the ground and joined Annie and Fuego. The three of them started rising toward the ridge. The big dog said, "I'm better. If I take it slow, I'll be able to get us over this ridge and into the next canyon."

The instant Annie supported her, Izzy went limp. Her eyes closed. She gasped, "We... did it."

Fuego flew over and grabbed some of Izzy's black frizzy hair in his small claws and pulled toward the ridge two thousand feet above them. "Faster. You can't go slowly. I did slow our pursuers down some. I beat them, but they're still coming. You have to hurry. We can't rest until we've crossed a lot of these mountains."

Izzy said, "Leave... me... behind."

Annie said, "No. You'd die. I won't leave you behind."

156

Only the humming of Fuego's wings filled the air. The intrepid band raced up toward the ridge. "You'll be safe soon."

The little hummingbird's wings buzzed. "We're getting you to safety. I met an eagle. She's preparing help for us, but you have to get there. Our enemy won't be able to follow us in these mountains, and we'll have help."

Izzy gasped, "An eagle?"

Fuego said, "A different kind in every way from Tuffy's sister. This one helped me."

Annie said, "That's good. It looks like we're going to get another thunder and lightning storm. Is it going to be safe to be going over ridges in that kind of storm?"

Izzy answered, "No, that's another reason to hurry. The only good thing is the storm will make it harder for the enemy to find us. Don't worry about me. Get to safety."

A gust of turbulence accented those words. Annie said, "I'm sorry, but I'm saving energy by not moving air with us. It's going to get rough."

Izzy said, "Do what you have to do. If you spot a stretch where I could run again, I've caught my breath. I could give you a bit of a break."

Fuego said, "We're almost over this ridge. Once you get over it, drop down below the top of the ridge and follow it into the middle of these mountains. Go west before you meet that tallest peak. You'll cross another canyon and a ridge. My new eagle friend will be watching for you. I'll go back and slow them down again." He let go of Izzy's hair and turned back. *I've been working too hard. I've got to refuel again.*

Izzy asked, "When will we see you again?"

157

"This will take me a while. I've got to get more fuel and check on the enemy. If they are over the ridge by the time I check on them, I'll just have to teach them to go slower. That'll take me a long time. I'll come find you in about thirty minutes."

In a hesitant voice, Izzy asked, "What if you don't come back by then?"

"That would mean I'm having lots of fun. You should go to where I told you as fast as you can. I trust the eagle. She and her friends will keep you safe."

The fearless little hummingbird buzzed back down into the canyon looking for late season flowers. Fuego watched for their telltale colors. If he didn't find any quickly, he'd have to just go with what fuel he had.

A more reasonable voice in his mind suggested not worrying about going back to fight. Fuego laughed at his own thoughts. *Those flying things are fun to fight, and I want to be sure they're slowed down enough.* The sooner he went to check on their pursuers, the better he'd feel.

I beat them once. I'll beat them again. I'm a good guy, and good guys always win.

~**********~

The helicopter pilot reported in to his commanding officer. "Sir, a crazy pyro hummingbird has damaged one of our helicopters. He has also taken out a number of our drones. Just now, an eagle joined him, and we lost two more of our helicopters. What are your orders?"

"It's just a tiny bird. Can't you get rid of it?"

"Sir, none of my weapons can target it or the eagle. The drones

158

have been chasing it and exploding near the bird, but none seem to have injured the bird. It changes directions too fast for them. Do you want us to continue our search for the dog and woman?"

"First, yes, I don't care how much equipment you lose. Just get me that dog. When you find the dog, be very careful. It's more dangerous than that tiny bird. Do not hurt the dog. I repeat, if you value your job, life, and the lives of anyone you care for, don't injure the dog. Once the dog gets tired enough, it's just a normal dog. Until then, it can control gravity. Second, we have examined the video of the battle with the tiny bird. The explosions have hurt it. We are sending in reinforcements. They will be there soon."

The pilot hated his job. He thought of an idea. "Why do we need this dog? Don't many fish control gravity and use it to move to and from spawning grounds?"

The boss's tone of voice left no doubt about what he thought of the pilot's idea. "That's a stupid idea. Fish are stupid and have no thought of how they control gravity. They have been useless as experimental subjects, but they have tasted good. We must have the dog."

Many thoughts raced through the helicopter pilot's mind. First and foremost, he wished that he'd never left the military. Working for this NGO was terrible. The other thought brought up a question. "What about the young woman we are tracking?"

"What about her?"

"We were told to find them and capture the dog. What are we supposed to do with the woman?"

"Kill her. No, no. What am I thinking?"

The pilot sighed in relief at the apparent change in orders.

"Absolutely do not kill her."

The pilot smiled for the first time in a long time. *Finally, I've got some good news.*

The voice continued. "She's in the mountains and on the edge of a wilderness area. Just wound her. The animals of the area can finish her off. She has caused us many problems. We will review how painful her injury was from the records and reward you for the most pain you can cause her. Be creative."

The pilot gasped. "That's terrible, Sir. I won't do it."

"Too bad. You were a good pilot."

The helicopter exploded.

Chapter Fifteen

Pooh's Remarkable Discovery

Birds of different species understand each other's calls and work together to defend against threats.

Aneroid Lake is in the Wallowa Mountains of northeastern Oregon in the middle of a wilderness area. Those mountains are all around 7,000 to 10,000 feet tall. Aneroid is in the middle of a valley called a cirque valley that was created by a glacier. The lake is only forty-five feet deep, and it is slowly getting filled in. Eventually, it will be just another alpine meadow. Roger Lake was a nearby lake. During the author's lifetime, it has evolved from a lake with many fish to a large shallow pond surrounded by marsh. It is closer to being just another meadow.

Pooh followed Coyote out of the crowd. The voices followed him.

"What's going on?"

"Who's the bear?"

"Did you hear? Coyote has asked him for help."

"Wow, that bear must be awesome."

The words echoed in Pooh's mind. He caught up to Coyote. "What are you up to?"

"Okay, I followed you and your dad up the trail. I wanted to get past the place where the wolves were. By myself, the wolves would've smelled me, and I wouldn't have been able to get past them. I figured to let them get distracted by the two of you, and I would sneak past."

Pooh said, "I knew it."

Coyote continued, "Then, things changed. After those deer displayed their special ability by moving fast, I saw you move your paw blazingly fast. I saw you help the pika. I didn't know what would happen with the wolves, but, yes, I did expect I would get past them. I also wanted to see what you could do. Pooh, you are very special. If there's trouble coming here, I want you with me."

"Oh, so you're still just watching out for yourself?"

"I always do, but it's more than that. This eagle is worried. I don't know if you know any raptors, but they don't get worried. They always figure that they can take care of anything. You saw all of the animals gathered here. What's happening up here is special. My mother told me what life used to be like for us wild animals. Things are changing. I don't want these animals hurt. I like what's happening up here. I want it to continue. I want you to hear what the eagle has to say. The people up here need you. You'll be a good friend for them. You're good at thinking and caring."

"I think too slowly." *Some of these animals could be my friends?*

"Pooh, you're a silly old bear. You don't give yourself enough credit."

The little bear didn't know what to say. Instead of responding, Pooh asked a question. "Why didn't they wake up the owl?"

"No one, and I mean no one, wakes up Owl."

From above them, perched on a branch, the eagle said, "Coyote, I talked with a mighty warrior. A mighty hummingbird Fuego fought against many enemies. He's trying to help his friends escape. They are being chased by many strange things. Those things are coming through the air and through the forest after them. I need to go back and help. If they manage to fight free, they'll fly over the ridge above us."

At those words, Pooh scratched his head. "Coyote, you should go back to make certain all the animals are ready just in case the strange things come here. Eagle, can you take me closer to where they'll be?"

The eagle responded by taking flight. In a few powerful wing beats, he soared into the air.

Coyote said, "And, Pooh, this is why I wanted you here. I'll go back and warn the others. I'll get them ready to help you. We might have to wake up Owl. I really hope she's already awake."

Pooh started running. *I wish I could fly. This is too slow.* Pooh had forgotten how sore his feet were. Running reminded him.

Boulders, brush, and trees got in the way. Pooh couldn't go faster. "Eagle, slow down."

The little bear thought. *Flying must be like what the fish do with gravity. Flying must be floating with movement. If I could do that, I could fly.*

The eagle kept going and getting farther ahead. The route the eagle took Pooh led him around the big tree. They came to a small beaver pond. On the far side of it, a small waterfall splashed into the calm water. One of the fish floated up in a ball of water and splashed down into the pond.

If only I could float like that, I could go faster.

Pooh's feet felt better. *The ground must be very soft here.* He tried to run faster, but no matter how fast he moved his feet, he couldn't move faster. *That's strange.*

He moved down along the edge of the stream below the dam.

"How much farther?" The little bear looked up, hoping to see something. Moving his head almost made him lose his balance. Pooh held his arms out to help keep from flipping. He didn't think about what flipping meant.

A few tree trunks angled across the stream to join the massive tree to his left. Through the gaps Pooh couldn't see much, but the sky looked darker. "Slow down, Eagle."

The eagle side slipped and soared back toward him. "Why are you so slow?" The eagle tipped her head down toward Pooh. "Why are you running in the air?"

Huh? Pooh looked down at his feet. Doing so made him flip. *I'm floating.* The little bear landed flat on his back on the ground.

The eagle asked, "What are you doing, you silly bear?"

I don't know. Pooh scrambled up on to his hind feet. "Where are the hummingbird's friends coming from?"

A gust of wind caught the eagle. "It isn't too far down to the lake. They'll come from over the ridge above the left side of the lake. I'm going over the ridge to check on them."

Pooh gazed after the departing eagle. *In a good story, the eagle would return safely with them, and I'll have lots of new friends.*

I should find someone to relay the eagle's information. A buzzing sound drew his attention to an old tree. Pooh lifted his nose into the air and sniffed. His stomach rumbled. *Honey. Honey.*

~**********~

Fuego flew back to the location where the vegetation looked different. All the way up the canyon, Fuego looked carefully for any of the flying or walking machines. *If I hadn't beaten them in that battle, they would've been here by now. I don't see any of them. My friends should be safe.* Spots of blackened foliage stood out to him. *How would there be just spots of fire?*

The warmth of the air in the bottom of the canyon felt great. Happily, Fuego looked for food. The bright colors of flowers rewarded his search. Fuego buzzed around, filling his tank with fuel. *This is a great place. This should be a resident hummingbird's territory.* A faint buzzing answered his thought. *I've got enough in the tank. I better go before I get in a fight with another hummer.*

Fuego didn't want to leave. The other hummer might think he'd frightened him. *I've got to go. This is too important.* Steadfastly, he ignored the sound of another hummingbird. Fuego kicked his speed up. He drew nearer to the ridge above him.

Fuego's sharp eyes caught a glint of metal in the trees above him. *They've made it over the ridge. I could light the trees on fire. That chipmunk wouldn't like me setting the forest on fire.* The little hummingbird ignored the easy choice of burning the trees.

He didn't see any more glints of metal, but Fuego heard the buzzing noises of the flying machines. He moved farther up and closer to the trees. In the back of Fuego's mind, he thought of his friends. *I'm so glad my friends got over the next ridge. By now, they'll be even farther away. If the eagle's right, they should be safe.*

~**********~

Pooh stood on his hind feet with his nose in the air. He heard the bees and smelled their honey. At his stomach's urgings, Pooh thought of nothing but the honey. Pooh forgot those in need of help. He forgot about Coyote bringing others to help. The tree in front of him had to be the honey tree, but how to get to the honey? That was his problem. Pooh scratched his head thinking about the problem.

This isn't an easy tree to climb. If only I could float again. I would use my claws on the tree and easily get up to the honey. Hmmm, how did I float before?

The little bear thought some more about the problem. *I was thinking of fish floating and thinking it would be so nice if I could float like them.*

As he thought, Pooh had been keeping one eye on his surroundings. The last time, floating had surprised Pooh. This time, he watched for the first indications of floating.

Movement caught his eye. *I'm moving.* Carefully, Pooh kept thinking of how fish floated and used his paws to guide himself up the tree.

The sounds of the bees grew louder. Pooh's stomach rumbled louder. Pooh said, "Quiet stomach. You're going to alarm the bees." Bees hadn't bothered Pooh much at Farmer's beehives, but there wasn't any need to warn them before he started eating.

Pooh spied the hole the bees flew in and out of. The little bear licked his lips in anticipation of his feast. Keeping his floating self anchored to the tree with three paws, Pooh lifted one paw to reach into the hole.

"Pooh, what are you doing?"

The little bear forgot about fish floating. With a lurch, Pooh started falling. He scrambled with his claws against the tree trunk to slow his descent. "Oh, bother."

Below him, Coyote said, "Step back everyone. Give him room."

Pooh finished his fall with a thump. He landed on his rear end. The little bear fell over backward. Pooh saw Coyote and other animals looking down at him. "You're all upside down."

Coyote shook his head at Pooh.

The other animals all talked at once.

"This silly bear is supposed to help us?"

"What was he doing up there?"

"We aren't upside down."

"Your head is upside down."

Coyote asked, "What were you doing, bear?"

Pooh pointed toward the ridge. "I am supposed to be watching for them to come over that ridge. It's too far for me to see."

Pooh pointed at the top of the tree. "It's a better view from up there."

Coyote said, "Oh, and there just happens to be a beehive up there."

The little bear looked up at the tree. His stomach grumbled.

Coyote said, "I think your stomach knew about the beehive."

"Yes. I think it did." Pooh thought it a good idea to change the subject of the conversation. "Who are these animals?"

Coyote said, "They are ones Owl picked to help *you* take care of this problem. He said the tree will help also. He said to give it our all."

Pooh heard the accent Coyote put on the word *you*. The little bear scratched his head in thought. *How could a tree help? What am I supposed to do?*

Coyote looked hard at Pooh. "Come on, Pooh. Get on your feet. Everyone is counting on you. I know you can do this."

At Coyote's words, the little bear climbed up onto his hind paws. *He has confidence in me? This is what I have to do.* Pooh tapped on the side of his head, thinking hard. "First, I need to know what you can do."

Everyone started talking at once. Pooh held his paws up and said, "All of you know each other. Divide yourselves into groups based on what special things you can do." After a pause, Pooh added, "There's something else. Are there any birds here who can fly fast?"

Three peregrines spoke up, "We are the fastest. What do you need us for?"

Pooh said, "We need to know when Eagle is coming with the dog and woman. We also need to know if and when those strange things are coming. Can you three space yourselves out between here and the other side of that ridge?"

The female peregrine said, "Yes. We can do that. You want us to give you warnings and updates. We will do it."

The three falcons simultaneously burst into flight. In seconds, they were almost out of sight.

Pooh said, "Wow, they are fast." He looked back at the groups of animals. "Now, which ones of you can attack the strange things as they come over the ridge and that can quickly go up onto that ridge?"

A group of horned animals moved forward, and the other animals hurried out of their way. The biggest of them said, "We mountain goats will protect our territory."

Before Pooh could respond to her words, the goats bounded away, taking increasingly bigger leaps. In very little time, they had disappeared from his view.

Pooh continued asking questions and giving orders. The last group left. The little bear looked around. The only one still standing by him was Coyote. "What are you still doing here?"

Coyote answered, "I'm waiting for you to give me orders, and I'm thinking someone should make sure your stomach doesn't talk you into forgetting what you're supposed to be doing. Oh, and by the way, good job. You came through just like I thought you would. You, Pooh, are a great thinker."

At that, Pooh's stomach grumbled.

Coyote grinned at the little bear. "See? What did I tell you? If I wasn't here, your stomach would have you up there after the honey."

Pooh heard something up in the sky.

~***********~

Up in the plane, P'Nut felt a tug on his tail. His new friend threw him at the floor. P'Nut felt the last touch of the hand.

Immediately, the little squirrel started his vibrating. Something else hadn't let go of him. P'Nut's muscles prepared for battle.

P'Nut had expected to vibrate through the floor of the airplane. That didn't surprise him. P'Nut hadn't understood what below the plane was like. The little squirrel hadn't been bothered by jumping dozens of feet above the ground.

Towering clouds floated around him. The surfaces of the clouds changed shape as P'Nut watched. The beauty of the rapid changes could've been mesmerizing. *Where am I? What happened?*

The shock caused P'Nut to keep vibrating. Something else kept him from being mesmerized by the changing clouds. P'Nut felt paws climbing his tail.

Teeth bared, P'Nut looked at his tail. One weasel climbed his tail. Another weasel held onto its tail, and the third held the second's tail.

169

The first weasel said, "Now, we have you."

Good. My friend didn't have to fight them. That thought blazed as the weasel climbed closer. *Three to one, the odds didn't sound good.*

P'Nut said, "Say hello to the clouds."

The expression of the weasel changed. Its paws moved faster. It said, "What?"

Then it bared its teeth and lunged.

P'Nut laughed. He'd already made his move.

~**********~

Flying up and closer to the trees, Fuego heard the noises more clearly. At this distance, he could see the gaps between the trees. *The machines could fly down between these trees.* Fuego maneuvered closer, looking.

The noises grew louder. *Where are they?* Fuego revved his wing speed up and darted back. Six of the small flying machines buzzed up from the other side of the tree. The closest of them exploded with a boom. Shrapnel ripped into the tree.

Fuego darted down into the branches, keeping the trunk between him and them. Another exploded. He heard shrapnel hitting the tree trunk.

From behind him came more noises. Fuego wanted to attack, but a survival instinct kept him dropping farther into the tree. The noises grew louder and he heard more explosions. *I should've used a fireball.*

Chapter Sixteen

The Race

Years ago, I thought of how possibly in a distant future, scientists could learn how to turn quantum effects into macro effects. Quantum effects are, generally speaking, smaller than an atom. Macro effects are what you can see in normal life. I decided to use that idea in my books. Just two weeks later, I stumbled across a scientific study proposing laying the groundwork to turn quantum effects into macro effects. There are now actually real quantum effects that have been turned into macro effects. Crazy, right? P'Nut's vibrating is borrowing from a quantum effect called tunneling.

Two types of energy are potential and kinetic. The boulder resting on top of a cliff has great potential energy. A boulder falling or flying through the air has great kinetic energy. Pushing the boulder off the cliff applies force to the boulder, increasing its energy and changing the potential energy to kinetic energy.

May you always have the force you need.

P'Nut tapped one of his cufflinks three times. *Bond told me things will attack those nearest me.* Just in time, P'Nut realized something. *These things will leave me but not be able to attack anything touching me.* Just in time, he stopped vibrating.

The wind and cold hit him. A high-pitched whining cut through the noise of the wind. P'Nut tumbled. He felt the pain of a bite.

The little squirrel felt the weight of the weasels disappear. The high-pitched whining died away. *Those cufflink things did their job.*

P'Nut's natural ability to jump long distances took over, and he stopped tumbling. Far, far below him, P'Nut saw... He wasn't sure what it was. There were large areas of green and some very small blue spots.

A memory came to P'Nut. He recognized what he saw from a similar scene in a movie. *Wow, I'm very, very far above the ground. Cool... It's cold. I'm freezing.* P'Nut shivered and curled into a tight ball.

~**********~

Pooh looked up at the sky. "Coyote, do you hear that noise?"

"Yes. It's been growing louder."

"My foster parents said that planes make that noise. I think they are machines. Can you call out to the nearest peregrine and ask them about it?"

Coyote responded to Pooh's question by turning toward the ridge and calling out a loud wavering question. He repeated the loud call and stood still, his ears pricked toward the ridge.

~**********~

P'Nut shivered. *Bond should've warned me about this cold.*

Bond's voice interrupted his thoughts. "P'Nut, can you hear me?"

"It's cold outside the plane. You should've warned me."

"Do you have the crystal?" The crystal dangled from its chain. The little squirrel kept a firm grip on the chain.

"Yes, but I still think you should've warned me about the cold."

"Good."

The one-word answer irritated P'Nut. He scolded Bond. "Good that I am freezing and you didn't warn me?"

"Listen carefully. You jumped too soon. You are still a long way from Noah, but there is good news. Remember the very special dog I mentioned? You are very close to it. This is a very important change to your mission. The enemy is also going after the dog. The dog flies by controlling gravity. Can you see the dog?"

P'Nut wanted to keep scolding Bond for not warning him about the cold. The words "This is a very important change to your mission" reminded P'Nut. *I'm a secret agent.* He stopped scolding and searched for a flying dog. *Wow, this is a crazy thing. I'm looking for a flying dog. I hope it doesn't like chasing squirrels. I'll be in a terrible situation.* "Does this dog like to chase squirrels?"

"What? Chase squirrels? I do not know. Do you see the dog?"

Bond had always seemed calm and cool to P'Nut, but this time he sounded a bit exasperated by the questions. The ground below looked rough, very mountainous. P'Nut spotted the green of many, many trees. *Trees are good.* He kept looking. *Water. There are big bodies of water below me.*

One in particular was right below him. It had an unusual looking tree along one side of the water.

P'Nut did not want to fall into water. He could swim, but he didn't like water. P'Nut shifted his tail. *I can easily avoid the water. I'll head for that tree.* Things kept getting clearer as he fell. "How do you know I'm near the dog?"

Bond said, "I am using satellites above you. I can see you falling toward a mountain range called the Wallowa Mountains. I also see the dog and the woman with her. They are moving toward a lake that should be right below you."

~**********~

Coyote said, "They've spotted the dog and woman, and there's a squirrel falling directly above us."

Pooh scratched his head. *How did a squirrel get above us? It must've jumped from the big tree.*

"They say the squirrel is high above the top of the tree, but it's getting closer. They say the plane isn't challenging their air space. It's flying away."

Pooh sat on his rump. *This story is getting fun. I like it.* His stomach rumbled, and he looked up at the beehive high in the old tree. *Honey would make this story better. It makes everything better.*

~**********~

A closer explosion knocked Fuego back into a branch. Needles and smaller branches poked his tiny fragile body.

Fuego's heart raced. In one heartbeat, he noticed a calamity. His wings had caught in the small branches. The little hummingbird struggled to untangle himself. Fuego couldn't seem to breathe. The

174

smoke from the explosions didn't help.

A spider on one of the needles stared at Fuego with its many eyes. Terror pulsed through the little bird. He couldn't get it with his beak. *This one is big.*

Instinctually, Fuego went to blast it with a fireball. The memory of the chipmunk fought his terror. The spider didn't move. Fuego managed to get some life-giving air back into his body.

Fuego felt his wings slipping free. *There haven't been any more explosions. What are they doing?*

Fuego eyed the spider. *Now, I could get it.* The spider seemed to realize the danger and scuttled back into the needles.

Those machines had been like a spider waiting and watching for me. They had a plan to kill me.

Buzzing and humming of the machines came from all around him.

This tree is on a steep slope. There are other trees near it. Thought became action. Fuego buzzed down the trunk and under all its branches.

A terrible sight greeted him. At least a-half-dozen of the metal-human-like things stood on the steep side of the canyon. Fuego reacted first, buzzing between the tree trunks. The things lifted the long tubes.

They're going to shoot at me, but they're so slow. I could probably dart between them and get them to shoot each other. The buzzing of the other things interrupted his thoughts and half-laid plans.

Fuego pushed his velocity to his maximum. Explosions came from just behind him. He heard projectiles and shrapnel hitting trunks, rocks, and the ground.

Something felt wrong. *I should be going faster*. Swerving past some trees, Fuego buzzed out into the open. Below him the river rushed peacefully along the streambed. Behind him, came another explosion. Fuego tried to go faster, but one wing lacked something.

The resultant imbalance between his wings caused him to swerve. A deadly piece of shrapnel spun just past his swerving body. Fuego spied a horror. Above him, dozens and dozens of the small machines flew over the canyon. *I've got to go slow them down. They'll spot my friends for sure.*

Fuego tried to boost his speed. Instead, he slowed down. Rallying his energy, the little hummingbird fired off a fireball at the distant threats.

The little hummingbird tumbled. Fuego dropped down out of the sky. An updraft caught him and briefly lifted him up. Fuego tumbled and the whole world spun around him.

He tried to fire off another fireball.

~**********~

One moment Izzy went up, and the next she went down. Above her and Annie, the storm clouds grew darker. She heard the first rumble of thunder from the approaching lightning and thunderstorm.

Annie asked, "How are you doing?"

Izzy really did not feel like talking. She feared it would cause her to throw up. Then again, that might make her feel better. Izzy looked out over the ridge at the new valley. She stared with two purposes. Staring into the distance supposedly helped with motion sickness. It wasn't working. Izzy forced back the need to throw up. "Stop asking how I'm doing. Just get us past this ridge. Maybe you could land me in this valley. I could run for a while." *Could I run the way I'm feeling? This turbulence is getting terrible.* Izzy didn't add the other thought screaming in her mind. *Get us out of this storm that's coming.*

"Okay, I don't know about landing you in this valley. I don't think this is where we'll be safe, and I have bad news. I'm sorry, but I'm getting very tired. I don't think I'm going to be able to move both of us at the same time much farther. I could keep us going by allowing one of us to drop while boosting the other. I'll trade off. This might get rough."

What? Horror filled Izzy at the thought of what Annie's words meant. *Annie can't mean what I think she means.* A call from above lifted her gaze and distracted her thoughts. She stopped looking for where she could run to help lighten the work Annie did in flying both of them. "Do whatever you have to do."

An eagle said, "Hello. You must be Fuego's friends. Is he back in battle?"

Annie said, "Yes. He went back to check on our pursuers, and to slow them down again. How close are we to safety?"

"You're almost there. Keep going the same direction. Go across this valley you're coming up to. You'll see a big lake far down and to your left. Go over the next ridge, and you'll see our lake and tree."

They had been flying over many trees. Annie asked, "What's so special about this tree?"

"It is much, much bigger than any other. I was supposed to report back about your approach, but I'd like to check on your little fighter."

Izzy said, "Yes. Please go check on Fuego. I'm worried about him."

"Keep going. I see your pursuers back a ways. I'll check on your friend and help him slow them down."

Another louder rumble of thunder spoke of the approaching storm.

~**********~

Fuego felt the movement of the air columns lifting him and dropping him. An explosion lifted him out of his daze, and he looked up.

The ordered pattern of small flying machines over him had broken up. Smoke showed the location of the explosion. Small pieces of debris fell.

A familiar voice spoke to him. The eagle said, "You were a great fighter. Your friends are going to be okay. I'll go back and help them."

Fuego's heart warmed at the words. Did he say thank you? The little bird didn't know. He didn't see anything else. It seemed to have gotten very dark. The winds carried him up and down. He didn't know it, but he dropped lower and lower. At one point, he thought he heard multiple humming sounds.

~**********~

Pooh looked up. "You say the squirrel landed in the tree close to us?"

Thunder rumbled through the valley and echoed from the ridges. Movement caught Pooh's eyes. His nose confirmed it.

It was a squirrel, but a different kind than Pooh had known before. Another, different, booming noise from high in the sky distracted his attention. *That's a strange sound.* The squirrel moved closer and recovered Pooh's attention.

The squirrel made an impressive leap, landed on a lower branch and ran out to the end of it. The squirrel had on a fancy suit jacket and what looked like a white shirt under it. "Hello, hello. My name is P'Nut. I'm looking for a flying dog." The squirrel paused and lifted its nose before asking, "What is that wonderful smell?"

Pooh looked at the squirrel. *Why is his name P'Nut?*

Coyote said, "Hello, P'Nut. Don't get Pooh talking about or thinking about that smell. Oh, and we're expecting a flying dog and a woman to come over the ridge above this lake."

Pooh said, "It's honey. I agree it's wonderful, but unfortunately, Coyote is right. I shouldn't think or talk about honey. My tummy will get excited, and I might forget what I'm supposed to be doing."

P'Nut said, "I like the shirt you're wearing. It goes with your fur. Is it from a movie?"

The bear answered, "No, I don't think so, but it is from a book about Winnie the Pooh. Mine's just a different shade."

The squirrel said, "Actually, now that you mention it, Pooh, I remember watching a movie about a bear named Winnie the Pooh."

Coyote interrupted before Pooh could say anything in response. "Okay, you two are obviously much more sophisticated than I am, but I think we have something more important to talk about than clothes, books, and movies. If you two could listen, you might hear the report from the peregrines. The dog and woman are coming over the ridge, and we have trouble."

Louder and longer thunder rumbled. Pooh looked at the ridge. He saw movement but couldn't make out the details.

179

~**********~

Annie no longer kept both of them flying at the same time. She'd already left the backpack and bag behind. Her head hurt, but worse, her heart hurt. *Izzy told me to ignore how she felt and keep going.* Annie couldn't ignore Izzy's screams and other noises. Annie boosted one of them forward and up while at the same time letting the other one fall in an arc. *A good dog wouldn't do this to her.*

From behind them, Annie heard the noises of the approaching drones. *Where is Fuego?* With a lurch, she rammed herself up. The wind whistled past her. It felt good on her tongue hanging out of her mouth.

Izzy screamed again. It broke off with some gagging noises.

Annie winced at the noises her friend made. *Maybe I shouldn't worry about getting her to safety. Maybe, I should drop her onto this ridge and continue on. Maybe, the machines behind us would leave her alone. I hate hearing her noises. I want her to be safe and happy.*

The race to get to safety tore at the poor dog's heart. *I'm hurting Izzy. I know I am. I don't want to hurt her. I want to be a good dog.* Annie did the only thing she could think of. She let herself drop with a lurch and boosted Izzy higher and faster. Even just moving one at a time got harder and harder.

A peregrine falcon flying hard blasted past them. From behind and below came the sound of an explosion. A glance back revealed a small cloud of smoke, debris, and feathers.

Annie looked forward, away from the sacrifice and let Izzy fall again while boosting herself. Another falcon zoomed at her and blew past. Annie whined. She knew what she'd hear. Another explosion came from behind her.

The eagle flew up beside her. "How do you keep going? I can tell you're exhausted."

"I can't give up. I must save Izzy." In the distance, Annie spotted another falcon approaching. She cried out to the eagle. "No, stop the falcon. It's just going to die like the others."

The eagle said, "It is a raptor. We laugh at danger. Unfortunately, it doesn't have any special ability except to go very fast. They are doing what they can to help you. We will get you to safety."

The third falcon blasted by. Its voice almost lost in the wind. "Keep going. You are almost to safety."

Annie whined again and asked, "But, why? You're wild animals."

"Yes, we kill and eat others. It is the way of the wild, but with the changes, we have learned a new wisdom. We work together. Owl, the wisest of us all, has said to give our all to help you. For us raptors, this battle is fun."

From behind them came another explosion. Eagle said, "My head feels better. It is my turn."

Annie said, "Don't die."

Eagle said, "Not yet. I still can do more."

~**********~

The largest of the mountain goats watched the race going on above her. The dog and human drew nearer. The things chasing them gained, but the sacrifices of the falcons took out those closest to the dog. She shifted her cloven feet to get a better purchase on the nearly vertical cliff.

The velvety soft pad between the hooves of her feet responded to her movement by sucking against the rock. *My feet will not fail me. I am one with the mountain. We will repel the invaders.*

A nearby boulder wriggled, as she nudged it with kinetic force. She was careful not to nudge it too hard. She just wanted to be sure it was free.

She watched the eagle fly toward the onrushing things. Multiple of the things crashed together, resulting in an explosion and another shower of debris.

Some of the things shifted course to chase the eagle, but when the eagle flew away, they returned to chasing after the dog and human with the others.

She decided that the things were coming into range, and they were getting too close to the dog and human. The time had come to initiate her plan. Using her special ability, she used a massive shove of kinetic force to send the boulder zooming at the things.

It missed all of them. The boulder harmlessly arced up into the sky and then down into the mountain valley. A number of things responded to the threat by changing course toward her.

The mountain goat leapt, following her carefully laid out plan. Ahead of her, the rest of her band of nannies waited beside an avalanche chute filled with scree. Those small rocks were the elemental part of her plan.

Chapter Seventeen

A Drowning

Being a hero is different for everyone. For some, it is getting up to go forth again even when depression and fear weighs on them like bags of wet concrete. For some, it is ignoring the cuts of the unkind words and deeds to live a life of love and caring. For others, it is not listening to the crowd but seeking what is right and doing the right and not what is popular. Many of these are the unsung heroes. They don't get medals. There was no moment of glory, just a continual struggle to be who they would be-could be.

Then, there are those whose instinct is not to run away from danger. Running from danger is normal and wise. Those heroes don't think of what is wise for their own safety. For others, it is giving their all, even their lives, for those they love, friends, acquaintances, or just because they believe in the cause. The greatest act of heroism is in surrendering all, not just in the moment, but with premeditation, that others might have hope for a better future. These are those who are most often remembered. Let us also remember the unsung heroes and help each other to be heroes.

P'Nut said, "I see them." He added, "Ewww, that does not look fun."

The dog and woman followed torturous paths through the sky. P'Nut couldn't stand watching. Just seeing their motion made him sick. He turned his head away from the sight. Behind them and over the ridge, the little squirrel saw things flying through the air and exploding. *What's going on?*

Lightning flashed, and, after a few seconds, the thunder rolled.

~**********~

The nannie goats fired off more of the small rocks littering the avalanche chute. Above them, a few of the things exploded as they reached the ridge and ran into the rocks blasting at them. Debris rained down.

The dominant nannie could feel a headache coming on. *We need to rest.*

The other flying things veered around the nannie-danger-zone. Some went higher and others went to the right and left.

A lightning bolt hit the ridge above them. The tremendous boom of thunder followed right behind.

The dominant nannie decided her next move. *We should move over the ridge and get lower.* Before she could say anything, she heard an exclamation of pain.

"Oh."

One of the other nannies tumbled limply down the cliff. A growing roar sound pulled her view farther down the cliff. Strange, metal-human-like things roared up from below. One looked bigger than the rest. Flames jetted out from something on their backs. They jetted straight up the edge of the cliff.

"Everyone, get up and over the ridge to our next position. Go, go, go! Don't wait for me and stick to the plan."

Another exclamation of pain and another of the nannies fell. Down below, the metal things pointed long tubes at them. She didn't know what those things were, but she recognized the danger. *I've got enough ability left to throw two more clusters of rocks with this force.*

Instead of climbing higher with the rest, she jumped down nearer the scree and ducked into a nook behind a bulge of rock. Carefully, she watched where she placed her feet. It wouldn't do to slip on the small rocks.

Instantly, she lifted a small cluster of the rocks and, lifting her head to look over the bulge of rock hiding her from below, spotted the nearest of the things. She fired off her clutch of rocks. She pulled back. A headache pounded. *I can only manage one more attack.*

Ducking back, she repeated the same action with another of the things. The first thing had been hit, and it spun wildly before crashing into the cliff in an explosion.

Something pinged off the rock beside her. A rock chip lanced her shoulder. She waited behind her boulder for another opportunity.

~**********~

Pooh walked down to the lake. "I don't see very well at much of any distance. Where are they?"

A faint scream from over the lake gave Pooh his answer. He spotted something that moved in an arc down through the air. Rapidly, it or they came closer. *What should I do?* The little bear scratched his head.

Pooh blinked. He didn't understand what he saw. It was blurry. *They don't look like they are flying. Is this really the dog and*

185

woman? They are falling. Flying would be some kind of floating. Why would they be falling? I hope they're not dead. Why are they being chased? Maybe they could be friends. What will they have for me to do? Pooh's stomach must've caused the next question. *Will they have honey?*

He didn't have much time to think, and he thought so slowly, but an answer came to him. "Come on, Coyote. They're going to fall into the lake. They might need help."

Pooh was familiar with water. He liked playing with it and swimming in it. With a rush and a splash, Pooh charged into the lake. Even with his shirt and wonderful fur, he felt the cold of the water. At first, it felt good after the warm day.

~**********~

P'Nut looked at the unfolding situation. It looked a bit like a disaster. *I'm supposed to help. What can I do? I'm supposed to be helping the dog, but I can't help it in the lake.*

Bond's voice cut through his thoughts. "You are probably wondering what you can do. Before you failed to cause the chaos, I had a backup plan. You might've heard a loud boom earlier. It wouldn't have sounded like thunder."

"Yes, I did. What was it?" P'Nut heard a slight humming sound.

"It was a package being delivered to your location. It should be pulling up to you right about now."

~**********~

Annie struggled. Her head hurt terribly. It felt like it would explode. *I can't use gravity anymore.* She could see the tree and the lake below them. The ground, trees, and the water rushed up toward them very, very fast, too fast.

The thought of the water screamed in her mind. *We're falling too fast, and I'm dropping Izzy into water, deep water. Nooo. I don't care if my head explodes. I have to slow us down.* Somehow, without knowing how, Annie found just a little more strength.

With a jerk, they slowed. They started to move over the water but dropped with two big splashes into the water.

~**********~

Eagle flew over the developing disaster. She'd crashed dozens of the small things, but there were more, many more. *How should I use myself? Can I save them?*

Something else, a different thing darted down out of the sky toward the edge of the tree and the lake. *What's that?* It came down and hovered by a squirrel.

The remains of the nannie band had crossed back over the ridge. Eagle watched the strange, metal-human-like things flying up the other side of the ridge. She'd watched them kill some of the nannies. *They are more dangerous than the smaller flying things.*

He spotted one more of the mountain goats still on the other side of the ridge. *What is she doing?*

A brilliant flash of chain lightning reflected off the smaller, strange things flying over the ridge after the dog and woman. The rumbling boom of thunder shook her. *I've got to get down before lightning finishes me off.*

Dropping lower, she saw Pooh swimming out into the lake followed by Coyote. Big splashes showed where the dog and woman hit the water.

Multiple bolts of lightning struck the ridge. A down draft struck the eagle, and big drops of rain pelted her. She partially folded her wings and stooped. She dove out of the down draft in search of an updraft. Her speed increased. *I'll go lower into drier air before I decide what to do.*

~**********~

Pooh swam as hard as he could toward the two falling figures. *They're falling too fast. I can't get there in time.* Pooh didn't give up. He swam as fast as he could. Time for the little bear usually moved at a steady pace and only changed its speed when Pooh had to wait for honey. Time would crawl while he waited for the honey. He didn't really understand why it went so slow. It must've been because Pooh wanted the honey so bad.

This time, he didn't want the dog and woman to fall into the lake, but for whatever reason, time seemed to slow down for Pooh. Maybe, it was because he wanted to help them so much.

The two figures falling slowed their fall. *That's it. Slow down some more. I can get there in time to help.* The woman's body didn't look like someone awake and concerned about the fall. She looked unconscious. Pooh especially noticed when they slowed. Her body hung limply in the air.

The two figures continued to slow and started to change direction, but then, they dropped the rest of the way into the lake with two big splashes.

The water flew out, hitting Pooh. He ignored the splashes. He just blinked and kept going.

The dog bobbed back up to the surface. In a weak, voice she called out. "Someone get Izzy. She's down too deep. I can't get her."

Pooh looked down into the crystal clear water. He could see the woman. Bubbles still swirled and floated up from her falling into the water. Izzy's arms and legs drifted limply out from her body. Pooh dove after her.

~**********~

The nannie goat waited back in her nook. Anger boiled in her blood. Two of her band had died. These metal-human-like things would pay.

She heard the different roaring sounds lifting the things up the cliff. *I'm in just the right position. The biggest will be coming up soon.* She shifted her cloven hoofs to be sure she had them securely braced against solid rock.

Some of the roaring sounds moved past her, going higher. A quick glance confirmed her suspicion and solidified her plan. The metal-human-like things kept their gazes up. They didn't see her hiding, waiting. They kept close to the cliff.

She tensed her muscles as she heard the last one and the biggest coming. Shoving off, she jumped, her front legs held in tight to her chest and hind legs out back. The thing didn't have any face to show surprise. It started to lift the tube object. It moved too slowly.

Head down, she rammed her horns into its head-like top. Sparking and smoking started, but she kept moving.

Her hind feet rotated forward and up and kicked. Her horns slid free. She bounded back and down onto a spire-like rock sticking up.

189

She leapt again and glanced back to see the result. The thing spiraled and tumbled down into the cliff below. As she landed, she heard it explode.

~**********~

In the crystal clear water, Pooh saw Izzy slowly drifting deeper. *I need to get her out.* He remembered his human parents taking him swimming. *They taught me so much.* I had to learn to hold my breath when I put my face into the water. Humans and bears can't breathe water like fish do. If humans breathe water, they drown and die.

Fish swam below Pooh. They swam so effortlessly compared to his efforts. *It's getting hard to hold my breath.* Pooh saw bubbles coming up from Izzy's face. *Bubbles float. The fish in bubbles floated. I floated.* Once again, Pooh put things together.

Izzy stopped drifting deeper. She rose. Pooh changed direction and swam with her toward the surface. His head broke into the air. Wonderful life giving air. He exhaled and gulped in air.

Beside him, Izzy floated, limply, in a ball of water. Coyote said, "Pooh, you got her, but doesn't she need to be out of that water?"

Pooh said, "Yes, I think so."

The water bubble disintegrated. Izzy started to slip back below the surface of the lake, but Pooh had already swum to her. Before Izzy could slip back under the water, Pooh grabbed her upper arm in his mouth. Biting down hard enough to hold her, Pooh swam as hard as he could for the shore.

Pooh heard the dog say to Coyote, "Don't worry about me. I'll get to shore. Please help the bear."

The tired bear swam for shore dragging Izzy's dead weight through the water. *She's not moving. What can we do for her?* His thoughts swirled and rushed about, but he couldn't think of anything except for the one memory. Humans drown and die. *I can't think of that. I have to first get her to shore.*

Above the tired and worried bear, a strange sight met his gaze. The small flying things hovered well above the lake. They flew in a large circle shifting and following the dog.

~**********~

The eagle watched with approval as the dominant nannie goat destroyed one of the metal-human-like things. That was how she took some of her prey. She would hit them and... Her thoughts led her to action.

All around her the lightning and thunder intensified. *I really should be getting out of this storm, but this opportunity is worth the risk.*

The eagle half folded its wings into its side, pulled its legs and feet up flat against its tail, and rolled over. It resumed its stoop. The eagle dove faster and faster.

The rest of the nannies had taken almost all of the other metal-human-like things. There was one left.

The eagle adjusted its dive. Its dive rapidly approached one hundred and fifty miles per hour. Unfortunately, it didn't have enough altitude to get to its maximum speed of two hundred miles per hour.

She knew how hard she would hit it and what the results would be. She didn't know the force of her hit would be similar to the force

191

of a hundred and thirty-pound person hitting a wall at thirty some miles per hour. She didn't know her claw grip had the force of four hundred pounds to the square inch. She didn't have that knowledge, but she had one thought.

I'm going to rip this metal-human-like thing's head off or just smash it into the cliff. Simultaneously, she slammed into the metal-human-like thing's head-like top and squeezed, ripping her claws through the metal shell.

The impact twisted the head with a screeching and ripping sound, but the top didn't come off. Her claws caused sparking. The blow and damage twisted the thing into a spin.

The eagle went with the spin. She waited to release her hold at just the right time to both flap away and to fling the metal-human-like thing into a bulge in the cliff. An explosion behind her testified to her success.

She already looked at the rest of the small flying things. *I could easily catch them, one at a time, but...* She also remembered how they had the nasty habit of exploding. *What could I do?*

The small flying things buzzed below her. They flew in a large circle over the slowly swimming dog.

Something else caught the eagle's eyes. *That I could attack.* In the next moment she changed her mind. Whatever it was, it was a friend.

~**********~

P'Nut gazed in wonder at the long flat device hovering next to him.

Bond's voice asked, "What do you think of this gadget? Jump

onto it. In the front is a screen. It will show you how to get strapped in and how to control it."

P'Nut smoothed his suit with one paw. "Does it do anything?"

Bond's responding shout hurt the little squirrel's ears. "Does it do anything!? It will let you save the day for all of us and let you play the hero I know you love doing. Just get on it. There is not much time. You have to rescue the dog now or all is lost."

At those words, P'Nut stopped brushing his suit jacket and jumped onto the long flat gadget. He hopped up to the front and, after looking at the display, reclined into a padded spot. He tried not to get concerned when the padded spot molded to his body and held him tight.

The screen showed him how to maneuver by shifting his body. Two sticks for his paws to grasp controlled the guns. *Yes. I'm finally getting a gun like the fictional James Blonde.*

Lightning flashed and thunder rolled. The sky grew darker. P'Nut hardly noticed the sounds of splashing and distant explosions.

He studied the video on the screen and practiced his movements. Unless he was asleep, he never stayed in one place this long. "It responds similar to how my body moves when I'm jumping. This will be easy."

"Yes, I used videos of squirrels jumping to design everything. We are running out of time. Go get those drones."

The little gadget shot forward. P'Nut leaned into the motion. *I've got this.* On the lake, Pooh swam back toward shore pulling a human. The coyote swam beside them and seemed to be helping.

The dog swam farther out in the lake. Around her, a large, hundred-foot-wide circle of dozens of drones flew.

A lightning strike blazed nearby. Almost immediately, thunder boomed. P'Nut wasn't sure what he did, but the gadget he rode on rolled multiple times.

P'Nut reacted and its flight leveled back out. He hung upside down. It took him a fraction of a second to flip the gadget upright.

Some of the drones noticed him and split off the circle to buzz toward him. P'Nut started shooting. They exploded. He grinned. *I like this gadget. What else could Bond make for me?*

Bond's voice said, "P'Nut, I have a vehicle flying in to give you a ride to safety. I will remove you, the crystal, and the dog from the area."

P'Nut soon had his paws full of excitement. Even in the growing darkness, he could see the drones. As it grew darker, P'Nut couldn't make out all the details of the drones.

He figured anything flying over the lake must be a drone. Not all of the drones exploded. Some just crashed into the lake after he shot them. The storm raged around him, but P'Nut didn't care about it.

This is so much fun. He did an inverted turn and lined up for his next shot. A lightning strike lit up his intended target. P'Nut froze.

The eagle said, "You made short work of them. The dog has almost made it to shore. Well done."

P'Nut said, "Thanks. I wish there were more. That was too easy." *I'm glad I waited. I almost shot this eagle.*

He turned about to the shore. The scene he saw didn't look good.

At that moment, Bond said, "Uh, oh, this is not good."

194

Chapter Eighteen

The Enemy Attacks

There are some trees that use lightning to get rid of competition and vines growing on them. Also, other organisms use electricity, the movement of electrons instead of breathing. Imagine a tree with all of that and the ability to play with lightning. I wouldn't want to try to chop it down.

Pooh finished pulling the young woman out of the lake. He looked at her body. *She isn't moving.*

The young woman lay still. The water glistened off her dark skin. Her lips were gray. Black ringlets lay plastered against the top of her face. Pooh lifted his head and wailed. "What do I do?"

The splashing sound of the dog and Coyote grew louder.

Pooh said, "I failed. I think she's dead."

From the lake, the dog said, "No, no. I drowned Izzy."

Coyote said, "I'll be right there."

Rain drummed down on them. Lightning flashed, followed by the rumble of thunder

~**********~

An explosion came from high in the sky.

Bond said to P'Nut, "I am sorry, but the enemy has destroyed your ride. Take care of the dog and the others. Now, they are your team. The enemy seems to have figured out my involvement. I might lose contact for a while. You are in great danger. They have—"

At the loss in communications, P'Nut flew higher into the sky trying to spot the danger. The winds buffeted his gadget. A lightning strike revealed a larger flying machine approaching. A big swarm of drones surrounded it. After a couple of seconds, thunder rumbled.

P'Nut couldn't estimate the number of drones. There were too many. *It's my lucky day. This is going to be fun.* P'Nut remembered one thing from his recent gadget training.

He looked at the screen for the information about how much ammunition he had left. Eagerly, he turned toward the approaching force.

P'Nut looked again at the display. The information he needed was a red bar that shortened as he used his ammunition. The red bar was gone.

Oh, well, I guess that eagle was safe. Now, what do I do? He looked around for the eagle. The raptor had descended and looked to be landing on the big tree.

P'Nut accelerated back down to it. "Eagle, there are many more coming. I can't shoot anymore. What can we do?"

Eagle said, "It's too dark for me to see. Go find the dog and woman. Help them hide. The storm is breaking. It's going to get lighter out. You'll have to hide until after the sun sets. Deep into one of the tree's caves would be a good place to hide them. Hopefully, it will stay darker until you hide."

Before the eagle finished talking, P'Nut thought again of almost shooting the raptor. *This shooting isn't all fun. It's dangerous.* Sunlight poured through a gap in the clouds. Under the dark clouds, a bright rainbow appeared.

P'Nut remembered how his friends had said a rainbow was a promise and a new hope. He could really use hope. This sunlight would make hiding very hard.

A growing machine sound announced the approaching enemies.

~**********~

Pooh licked the woman's face. *Please wake up. Don't be dead.*

Annie licked her hand. "Izzy, wake up. Don't die. Please, don't die. I'm so sorry I dumped you into the lake. I tried to get you to safety. I wish I had died so you lived. I wanted to get you to safety. I should've set you down sooner."

Coyote laid his head on her chest. He didn't say anything. He just shut his eyes.

Another voice spoke, and Pooh recognized it. Stump the beaver said, "It's sad. I know this. If anyone stays underwater too long without breathing, you breathe water and die."

A device flew up, and from it, P'Nut spoke. "We need to hide the dog. The enemy is after the dog."

Annie said, "I can't leave Izzy."

Pooh said, "Coyote, what are you doing?"

P'Nut said, "We have to hurry. Coyote get off her. If the dog won't leave Izzy, we'll have to drag her with us."

197

Just then, a big owl flew up and landed not too far from them. "Well, I say now. You must be Pooh. Am I correct in assuming you drowned this woman?"

Pooh looked at the owl. *What?* "I don't think so. I dragged her out of the water. Did I do it wrong?"

Annie said, "No, Pooh, I'm the one who dumped her into the deep water. I drowned her. I'm a bad dog. I'm so sorry."

P'Nut grabbed his hair with both paws and pulled. "Can we stop talking? We need to hide the dog."

Owl said, "Well, well, I think it is too late to hide anyone. They are coming close enough to see all of us."

Pooh said, "Oh, bother. Coyote, get off her. We should try to get away. When I'm playing Pooh ball I always try no matter how bad it looks."

Stump said, "No, Coyote can't move. He doesn't like people knowing what he can do."

Pooh asked, "What can he do?"

Owl asked, "Am I right in assuming Coyote is trying to heal this young woman?"

Stump said, "Yep, you're right, Owl. I don't know if he can do it. She was in the water for a long time. She doesn't look good. I'm surprised Coyote is even trying. It makes him sick to heal some folks. This might kill him."

Pooh stared in surprise at Coyote. *He's really trying to help someone? He's risking his own life? Come on, you can do it.*

P'Nut said, "Okay, the young woman isn't going to hide. She might be dead. Good luck. Okay, we need the dog to hide. The enemy is after her."

198

Annie said, "No, I'm not leaving Izzy."

Pooh said, "Oh, bother. You should try to hide."

Stump said, "I think those enemies are close enough. Owl, can Tree take a shot?"

Owl said, "Well, I say now. It does seem like a good idea. She responds best to you, Stump, although I surely don't know why. You cut trees down. Why would they listen to you?"

"Because I know and value trees, and they know it." The beaver patted the tree trunk by him and mumbled.

P'Nut said "I can't wait here all day. I'm going up to delay them."

Annie said, "Wait. Don't go. I'll hide if you don't go. Fuego went to try and delay them, but he never came back. I'm afraid he died."

Owl said, "Hold on until Tree gives it a try. She is a bit slow in understanding, but I think this will help."

The black clouds continued to move away. The rain had stopped, but there were still occasional rumbles of thunder in the distance. A bolt of chain lightning flashed out from the tree. Thunder rumbled. The bolt zig-zagged through the approaching enemy.

Some of the small things exploded, but too many kept coming.

P'Nut broke the disappointed silence. "Okay, we should go."

The biggest machine flew down toward them. A loud voice thundered down from big flying machine. "Give me the dog, and no one will get hurt."

Owl asked, "Well, I say now, who is the big know-it-all leaning out of that machine?"

Annie said, "It's the big boss. He isn't very nice. I better go with him."

P'Nut said, "No. Wait just a few seconds. Surely, we can come up with something."

An idea started to grow in Pooh's mind. Would it work? He really didn't like it. Pooh's stomach grumbled.

Eagle flew down to them. "I thought you should know something."

P'Nut answered first. "What?"

"I think we have help."

Fireballs and explosions made everyone look up. Pooh asked, "What is it?"

Eagle said, "There are at least a half-dozen hummingbirds attacking them. I will go to try to talk to one. Hopefully, I will not get hit by one of the fireballs. If Fuego was any indication of how hummingbirds fight, it is very dangerous up there."

The big flying machine had two big propellers on either side of it. The machine, a helicopter, shot away from the explosions. It went straight up into the sky.

P'Nut said, "I'll go up to see if there's anything I can do to help." He surfed off on his flat gadget.

Izzy coughed. Water gushed out of her mouth.

Coyote rolled off her and backed up. He laid his head back down and shut his eyes.

Izzy rolled over, coughing and spitting out more water.

Pooh gazed in happy surprise. *Coyote did it.*

Coyote mumbled from his prone position. "I almost gave up. She was very far gone. Then, I could feel her fighting. She's a fighter. I couldn't give up on her. I think she's going to make it."

Izzy pushed up onto her hands and knees. "What happened? Where are we?"

Annie said, "You're alive. I was so worried. I'm sorry I didn't take better care of you. I'm sorry I dumped you into the lake. I'm—"

Izzy interrupted her. "Whoa, I'm okay. I'm just very tired."

Pooh said, "That's great. Coyote saved you, but now, we should all get away from here."

Coyote said, "Leave me alone."

Owl said, "He needs to rest."

Izzy said, "Do I have to—"

Annie said, "The big boss is above us. If you are up to it, the bear is right. We should try to get to a safer place."

Stump said, "Come along with me. I know just the spot."

Above them, the explosions continued. P'Nut surfed down from the battle. "I have a wounded hummingbird. Can Coyote help him?"

He tipped the gadget slowly over and a hummingbird rolled off onto the ground. "They're fighting too close to the drones and getting hurt in the explosions. I'll be right back."

Coyote said, "It would be easier to eat it. Ah, it's so small. He isn't worth eating. I can keep it alive, but after the Moon goes down, it's no more mister nice guy."

Owl said, "Well, well, Coyote, you really should rest."

Coyote said, "Rest is for the dead."

Eagle half tumbled and half flew down to crash on the ground. "I think I've gotten hurt."

Coyote said, "Get in line."

Pooh had helped Izzy stand. She wobbled, but with his help she started to slowly walk.

The blasts of fire and explosions above them stopped. Pooh and Izzy looked up. A few hummingbirds flew up to them. P'Nut soared back with three more hummingbirds on his gadget. Above them, the helicopter began to come back down.

One of the hummingbirds said, "We've exhausted our abilities, but we destroyed the little machines."

Owl said, "Well, well, thank you. Your help was very well-timed. How did you come to our rescue?"

"A great fighter fell from the sky. We saw those he'd fought against and chased after them."

Izzy said, "Oh, no. That must've been our friend, Fuego. Is he okay?"

"No, I don't think he survived, but we got rid of all his enemies. He would be happy."

Pooh said, "I don't think so. I hear the biggest machine's coming back. Excuse me, Izzy, I need some honey." His stomach grumbled again.

Coyote said, "Pooh, what are you doing? This isn't the time."

Pooh didn't answer. He floated up the honey tree carefully using his paws to not float away. *Floating up and getting honey. It is so very simple, but will it work?*

Above the little bear, one little black cloud hurried after the storm.

Fear from what might happen if this action failed threatened the little bear's mental hold on floating. He still didn't understand how he could float, but he knew if he doubted, he would fall. *I need to focus on something that floats.*

Pooh looked up and spotted the small black cloud. To fight the fear and to focus, Pooh made up a song and began to sing.

Izzy asked, "What's the bear doing?"

Annie said, "I think he's singing a song."

Pooh sang. "I'm a little storm cloud, black and round. I am a little storm cloud, floating free. I'm a little storm cloud, black and round."

Owl said, "Well, I say now. What is that silly little bear doing?"

Coyote said, "I trust him. Honey's a problem for him, but I think he's got an idea. I tell you, Pooh's a thinker."

Coyote's words reached Pooh. The little bear felt a surge of confidence and hope. He heard the buzzing of the honeybees and saw their hole. He lifted a paw and jammed it as far into the hole as he could.

Pooh pulled out his paw. It had bits of bark, a few bees, and most importantly some honey and honeycomb. Pooh's stomach rumbled in anticipation. "I'm sorry, but you'll have to wait. There's something important I need to do. Now, don't distract me. I have to focus." His stomach rumbled just a little.

He pushed away from the honey tree and floated faster and faster around the trunk. From below he heard Owl. "I say. What is that silly bear doing?"

Coyote said, "Hush."

The little bear heard the angry bees gathering. *I hope they can understand me.* "You bees can't get me. I'm going to eat all your honey."

The bees must've understood because they buzzed louder. To Pooh, they seemed to be saying, "Get the robber."

A cloud of bees had formed. It was a big mass of them. They

buzzed after Pooh. He shifted course and focused on moving faster. *It's working.* The little bear had no idea how he did it, but it fit his memory of other times he'd done special things. *I need to think hard of doing the new thing and not get distracted.*

Pooh heard the buzzing of the bees chasing him, as both he and the bees flew faster. He also heard the helicopter over him. It was getting closer.

The little bear saw a big man moving in the doorway of the helicopter. Pooh couldn't see everything, but what he did see filled him with confidence. He picked up speed with the bees in hot pursuit.

Pooh remembered how superheroes flew. He held both paws out in front of him. He aimed right for the doorway of the helicopter.

The big man must've seen him coming. He started shutting the door of the helicopter.

Pooh managed to go faster. *I'm going in. How I'm doing it, I don't know, but that doesn't matter.* The wind of his flight ripped a small bit of honeycomb covered in honey off Pooh's paw.

Luckily or unluckily, it hit Pooh's nose. His stomach rumbled very happily. Pooh's eyes went cross-eyed trying to look at it.

Pooh forgot to keep focused on aiming at the helicopter. *Just a very small taste wouldn't hurt. I can still do this.* Pooh remembered how he'd always thought just a taste wouldn't hurt. *I've never been able to stop eating until it's all gone. My stomach always controls me.*

The little bear clenched his jaw shut just as his rebellious tongue reached for the very small taste. His eyes went wide at the pain of biting his tongue.

Pooh stubbornly ignored the pain and the little, tiny taste of honey on his nose. He refocused on the closing door and flew in through the door followed by the angry bees just before the big bald man shut the door.

Chaos ensued. Pooh swatted the man with his honey covered paw. *What a waste of wonderful honey.* Pooh bumped and crashed around in the helicopter. He managed to get some honey on the man in the front of the helicopter.

The big man screamed and swatted at the bees. The other man started screaming. The helicopter tipped.

In the chaos, screaming, and struggle, the big man managed to get the door open again. He jumped out. Pooh zoomed out right behind him. Only some of the bees managed to follow.

The bees that followed must've decided they'd had enough and flew back toward the honey tree.

Pooh's tongue managed to lick the bit of honey and honeycomb stuck on his nose. The little bear sighed at the sweetness. His stomach rumbled happily. Pooh also forgot to focus on floating. He fell.

Down below him, something white floated over the big bad man. Below them lay the lake.

Usually, Pooh didn't think very fast. This time, maybe from the influence of that very small taste of honey or the idea of the rest of the honey getting washed off his paw by the lake, Pooh's thoughts rushed. *I need to float again.*

Faster than he expected, things changed. He stopped falling and floated. Above him, the helicopter seemed to be having trouble. Its engine whined. It wobbled back and forth. *Those bees I left must be causing trouble.*

It veered away and crashed into the ridge with a great explosion. Pooh floated away from it as fast as he could. He dropped down.

Everyone below him turned their faces up toward him. Pooh landed by them and held his paw up. "Would anyone like a taste of honey?"

Author's Note

Thank you for joining me on this journey with Pooh, P'Nut, Fuego, Annie, and Izzy.

Before you read any farther, please use the QR code below to write a book review of *Pooh and P'Nut* on Amazon. I would greatly appreciate your taking the seconds to support me in this way.

Author's Final Note

Hello, everyone. I'm author TLW Savage, otherwise known as Tim. My real name is Tim Walker. I borrowed the last name of Savage from an ancestor of mine. It gives me a much more unique pen name and will make it easier for you to find my other books.

I hope you've enjoyed this novel *Pooh and P'Nut* as much as I enjoyed creating it for you. I hope this story touches you the same way as the first book in this series, *Tuffy*, touched one of my readers. Their review also touched my heart. That fan got just what I labored for all my readers to get. I have striven to give you a delightful mix of heart, humor, and adventure—a book that will stay with you for a long time.

Below are two different ways of contacting me. I'm still answering all my email. Also, for any of my fans with ideas they'd love to see in future books, please share your thoughts. If I use your ideas, I'll give you credit for the joke, character or whatever the idea was.

You're all amazing, and it was my privilege to share my story with you. Take care. I love you.

TLWalker@TLWalkerAuthor.com is my email

TLWalkerAuthor.com is my website. I'm planning on making a major upgrade to it as soon as I can afford it. Find me on Facebook as TLWSavage. Be sure to message me on Facebook and identify yourself as a fan. I use to work in Cyber Security, and I'm careful about accepting new friends on Facebook.

TL Walker, Author

Tim began writing in Olympia, Washington. A grandpa, he and his wife enjoy their children and grandchildren. He loves making great food and gets even more enjoyment from watching family and friends eat the food.

He began creating stories at an early age. One night, his seven-year-old sister woke up screaming, and he went to comfort her. On the spur of the moment, the twelve-year-old Tim created a fantastical story for her, calming her with attention-grabbing details.

Tim's fascinated by everything from flowers to Genghis Kahn and from sand to the universe. He finds people particularly interesting. He's always on the watch for interesting features and personality quirks for use in a story. If you come to his website and visit, you might find yourself in a book. He has been active in local writing groups and a beta reader for other writers.

Currently, he is also doing Writer Camps. He loves helping others.